A Man For Beth

A Christian Romance

By

Ruthie Madison

A Man for Beth

Published by Unique Pen Press
Cover by Madison Book Cover Designs
Images by Zastavkin@Depositphotos.com

voyagerix@Depositphotos.com

www.ruthiemadison.com

One

Empty pints of ice cream lay strewn over Beth's floor as she moaned in bed over a tummy ache. Her mother stopped by her room, shaking her head, but Beth didn't care.

"You need to stop feeling sorry for yourself!" her mother said.

"Why? No one wants me."

"No, they won't if you're going to binge after every bad date. That's how you gain weight."

Ann walked in and picked up the empty cartons as Beth smirked. "At least ice cream doesn't abuse me."

"Do they abuse you at your new job??" She tossed the cartons into the wastebasket, then sat on Beth's bed. "You need to start living life."

Why did Beth come home after the fiasco with Brad? Or was it Drew? It sickened her. Drew used her. Hadn't she learned her lesson the first time? No man wants you because you're a fat pig, an accusing voice told her. How could she live life with that reminder?

"I have an idea!" Her mother jumped up, her voice filled with excitement. "Why not join a gym? It would do us good!"

Beth rolled her eyes. She didn't want to work out. Lifting weights and doing curls sounded hard. She had seen the episodes of the Biggest Loser where the contestants struggled to exercise. But at the same time, a strong overwhelming desire came to the forefront of her mind. A few tears fell. "Okay. I guess."

"Great!"

Hearing her mom humming a happy tune as she walked away reminded her of a verse. “A fool singing a happy tune to a sad person—rats! I need to get into the Bible more.” Since she left Montana, she’d lost the joy of fellowship. How was Julie doing since her rape? “I should give her a call.” Beth glanced over to her Bible on the stand. “But first the Bible.”

****

The building itself intimidated her as Ann parked her red car in the parking lot of NorCal Gym. The tall two-story building spanned half a block. As they walked to the entrance, Beth cringed. The treadmills taunted her.

Her mother led her in and waited at the front desk.

A bubbly young woman behind the counter greeted them. “Hi! Welcome to NorCal Gym. What can I do for you today?”

“I’d like to sign my daughter and me up for membership.”

Beth groaned inwardly at her mother’s enthusiasm.

“Would you like a personal trainer too?”

“Yes!”

“No!” Beth shouted, hoping the lady would hear her.

Her mother glanced at Beth. “You’ll be okay, Beth. He can help you get in shape.”

“We have a two-for-one deal. The regular price for a one-year membership is ninety-nine dollars.”

Beth’s skin tingled in shock. “Ninety-nine?” She expected far less. “That’s too much, mom!”

“Nonsense. Do you accept checks?”

"And credit cards."

Her mother removed her Visa card and handed it to the perky woman behind the desk. The woman gave them forms to fill out. "We need to have an idea what your needs are." She swiped the credit card, had her sign the receipt, and gave her a copy. "Here's your card."

Ann dropped the card in her purse, then they walked over to a row of chairs to fill out the forms.

Sometime after they filled it out, a big beefy man wearing a white tank and gray sweat pants stood in front of them. "Which one is Beth Miller?"

Her mother bounced up and down and pointed to Beth. "Her!"

Beth wanted to run. Her ears and eyes felt hot. Oh God! This can't be happening! She shoved her hands into her shorts pocket. "Mom."

The sexy trainer stared down at her and smiled. "Nice to meet you, Beth." He didn't see her flush. Maybe he was used to it. "I'll show you your lockers first." He led the two to a set of lockers on one side of the room. "The key cost a dollar."

Beth's mom gave him a dollar and he went to get a key.

"You're embarrassing me, mom."

"I'm sorry, sweetheart. I'm excited we're here."

If she committed to coming here for a year, she didn't know she could handle it. She never had to work out before. She had a good figure prior to a relationship with an occult member. She shuddered. She blamed herself for gaining weight, but she had no desire to get in shape. Couldn't men love her for her and not her outer beauty? She glanced around, and her skin tingled when she noticed two men lifting weights. She smiled.

****

She noticed him. Stan turned his attention back to the weights. He couldn't allow another woman to break his heart.

"I think she likes you, Stan," his friend Larry said.

"Me? We haven't even met." He picked up a 100-pound weight and lifted. "She probably thinks men are jerks." And he didn't blame her. Although since becoming a Christian, he still needed an attitude adjustment. Did she know the Lord?

"No time like the present. Go and introduce yourself." Larry lifted 100-pound weights.

"I don't want to scare her." He had lost weight since his journey began six months ago. They could start out as friends, but he didn't want her to think he was coming onto her. She may have had bad experiences with men.

He had one with a woman. Laura was a beautiful woman, but her heart was not. She was ashamed to be in public with him. For the first two months, she seemed to accept him as he was—overweight. He thought she had a heart of gold until he overheard her talking to a friend on the phone.

"Stan won't lose the weight. He told me that is who he was, and he acted real macho…Dump him..." she had paused. Did she suspect he was near? He quickly hid when she glanced around the room.

He fell on his knees and cried but straightened up. Real men don't cry, his father had told him. They pray.

Stan's father was a God-fearing man. He respected him, but after his father died, he lost hope in God. He walked away from God and the Catholic Church.

The woman dropped the weights she had used and wiped the sweat off her brow.

She had a hard life too.

Stan didn't doubt she had a hard life. She reminded him of himself six months ago.

You could help her.

We can be friends.

Two

As Beth and her mother finished working out, she took a deep breath. "That was hard." She followed her mother to the changing room.

"But you did it! You made it through your first day! I'm proud of you."

"I guess you want me to keep it up."

"We both can."

Beth stared past her mother. The two men were walking toward the lockers. Her heart raced. Oh God, please don't let them talk to me! She wiped her sweaty palms on her leg and kept her eye on her locker.

He was there. Was his locker near hers? No! Through the smell of sweat, she detected a hint of Old Spice cologne. Did he come here to attract women? She eyed him. He looked amazing!

"Hi." He cleared his throat. "Stan. And you are?" He closed his locker door.

Was he talking to me? She wanted to run, but her feet froze. She tried to speak, but nothing came out. Over her shoulders, her mother smiled.

"Go ahead and say hi," she whispered, coaxing her on.

"Nn…nice to meet you. Beth."

"Beth? I love your name."

Her heart fluttered, and she glanced away.

"Would it be okay if we can be friends?"

Friends? Yes. That would be good. She offered a small smile. “Sure.” Her heart wouldn’t slow down. He offered friendship, not a relationship. Get a grip, girl!

“Is this your first day here? I haven’t seen you here before.”

She nodded. She couldn’t let him know it was her mother’s idea to join the gym. What would he say if she did? “Um…yes.” She gave a nervous laugh. No doubt he joined the gym long ago. He had muscles on him, but not as muscular as body builders. He wasn’t as overweight as she was but had meat on his body.

He stared at her, but it wasn’t gawking. If anything, his eyes showed understanding. “It will get easier. Don’t give up.”

Her mouth dropped open, then she closed it. “Thanks.” She stared at her feet. An accusing voice told her he would walk out laughing at her, but she ignored it. Her heart warmed. Was her skin flushed? She hoped not. “You’ve been there?”

“Pardon?”

“Overweight like me?” Did girls reject him the same way others reject her?

“Yes. Working out is hard, but if you keep at it and not give up, you’ll reach your goal. I hope I see you again.”

Now she was sure her face reddened. She never met a man who wanted to see her again. “Me…too.”

“I have to return to work. By the way, where do you work?”

“Book Ends Book Store.”

His eyes grew big. "Really? You're my competition! I work at Jan's Book Deals—well, we sell used and new books."

"I just started working at Book Ends."

"As friends, would you have lunch with me?"

She could hear a squeal from her mother, but doubt plagued her mind. She liked him, but he wasn't her type. He wants to be friends! Don't make a big deal out of it.

"I promise nothing else." He smiled.

"Okay. As friends."

"Great! Do you like Wendy's?"

"Yes."

"Can I pick you up?"

She giggled. She knew what he meant but she had to say, "Can you lift a 190-pound woman?"

He chuckled. "Not yet."

"I'll meet you there." They had one Wendy's and she knew where it was. She wasn't ready to ride with a man she just met.

"12:15 too early?"

"No."

"See you then."

Stan followed his friend out of the gym. Her heart hammered. She wished it didn't. She couldn't keep from staring at him.

"Oh, Beth! This is wonderful! He is interested in you–"

"As friends," she reminded her mother.

"It's a start! I think he would be right for you. See if he knows Jesus. Thank you, Lord!"

Beth raised her eyebrows. "What are you thanking Him for? Stan isn't my type."

"What is your type? A tall lanky man…or a muscular man?"

Beth rolled her eyes. "First, Mother, I am not into dating, which is why I don't mind being friends with him. He seems nice enough."

She sighed. "Either he has issues too or he sensed you're not interested in dating. Maybe it's the way you came across."

"Came across? Really, mom! I talked to him, didn't I?"

"Sure, you did, but it's possible he detected it in your voice. Why are you suspicious?"

Beth tried to push the lump down in her throat. She didn't want to answer her mom. What could she say? If she lied, her mother would know, not to mention her mother taught her not to lie. The heat rose behind her eyelids. "I'm not suspicious!"

"Then what are you?"

"Please, mom! Let's not discuss it!" She took her gym bag and ran out to the car.

Their house was not in sight. She felt trapped. She could hail a taxi, but she would have to face her mother. It was Saturday, so going to work would not work. "I need a life." She grumbled, then slumped in her seat.

"Sorry, I upset you." The front door had opened on her mother's side and she sat up, not staring at her mother.

As her mother drove them home, she played a Steve Green CD. Her mother was nothing like Julie. They loved the Lord but didn't have a deep relationship with Him. Her mother never listened to praise music. Beth missed it. She could listen to it when she's alone but when she was with her mother, she couldn't. "I know what I'll do," she thought. "I'll lock myself in my room and listen to Julie True." She loved immersing herself in inspirational Christian music.

"I hope you don't lock yourself in your room!" Her mom parked in front of the house and locked eyes with Beth. "You hear me?"

"What do you want me to do? Play bingo with you?" Her tone was sarcastic, but she didn't care. Her mother embarrassed her enough. "Besides, I need to recharge in my room."

Gazing at her mother, she realized her mother didn't have a life. Ann worked full-time as a physical therapist. She had to because when her father passed away, he didn't have sufficient money for them to live on. They depended on a one-person income and her mother worked part -time as a receptionist while taking classes to become a physical therapist. Since his death, her life revolved around Beth. "We can play bingo later, if you want." Her voice softened toward her mother.

Ann gave a warm smile. "That would be great. I'll do some reading."

"What book are you reading?"

Ann giggled. "Just a short book about a foreign woman who moved with her mother-in-law to another country. Yesterday, I read about the sin cycles of the Israelites."

Beth understood her mother was reading the book of Ruth. It was Beth's favorite book. "Enjoy the book."

“Thanks, I will.”

“Don’t forget to pray.”

“I won’t.” She climbed out of the car and removed their gym bags out of the back. Carrying hers, she led her daughter to the house.

Beth closed the door behind her as her mother passed her room. Despite the fiasco at the gym, she enjoyed spending the morning with her mother. Beth worked from 9 a.m. to 6 p.m. while her mother worked two jobs. They rarely saw each other.

Why hasn’t she found a man to replace her father? Although not model perfect, her mother had a good figure. She wore her hair short because it would get in her way and it complemented her. Ann was a good catch for her father. She envied her mother. “I shouldn’t let myself go.” Thickness gathered in her throat. She walked to her mirror and stared at her 190-pound figure.

The leather-bound book on her nightstand caught her attention. Her mother had the right idea. “Should I worship or read?” The more she stared at the Bible, the more it invited her to partake of what was inside.

“Dear Lord, help me to see me as you see me.” Her mom was right. She didn’t trust men. How could she have a relationship with a man if she had issues? “I need your help.”

She opened the Bible

Three

Stan parked his car next to a white Toyota. Was the car hers? He couldn't imagine Beth driving a Nissan. At the gym, her mother slid right into a red Nissan, but he didn't see Beth climb in after her.

What drew her to him? A light? Perhaps she loved Jesus. Oh, he hoped so! He would pray for her while he waited in the car.

A worship song played on his radio, which was perfect to set the mood for prayer. He closed his eyes and prayed.

Time had gotten away. When he ended, the clock on his dashboard read twenty after twelve. He opened the door and jumped out as a heavyset woman walked toward the entrance. His heart did a number on him, but he reminded his heart they were friends. Besides the inner beauty, he didn't know why he asked her to lunch with him, but here he was.

****

Stan didn't appear anywhere. Did he say fifteen or fifty after? Was she early? She checked her watch as she waited in her car. Was I supposed to wait for him inside?

The time she spent worshipping and praising God went longer than thirty minutes, but God was worthy of her time. Her mom reminded her to ask him if he knew Jesus. Of course, she would. She continued to worship Him as she drove to Wendy's.

A white car raced past her. What was he in a hurry for? She got a glimpse of the driver having short brown hair. Was the driver him? Was he late? If so, she could relax. "I don't know why I am doing this!" Of course, she knew why. Her mother encouraged her to give him a chance. She had seen her off, saying, "Enjoy your lunch with Stan." She breathed easier when her mother didn't say date.

The same white car sat in Wendy's parking lot as she arrived. Coincidence? However, she waited, hoping if the car belonged to Stan, he would step out first. She watched. His head bowed down as if he was praying. A voice told her the man was Stan. She let out a squeal.

Here goes. She squeezed out of her car and walked toward the entrance.

"Beth?"

Her pulse quickened, and she shot a look toward the speaker. "Stan. Am I late?"

"No, we both are. Wow! You look wonderful after a workout."

She was certain she blushed. "Uh…thanks, but I don't feel wonderful."

"Your cheeks are glowing." He smiled. "Shall we?" He held the door open for her.

"Oh that?" She giggled. "I guess my time with Jesus does that."

His eyes widened. "You know Jesus?"

"Do you?" His question promised hope.

"Yes, ma'am, but not all my life."

"Oh, well," she said, following him inside, "I've known Him most of my life, but I strayed years ago."

***

His heart warmed. She is! He desired to know her here was his chance. "Where would you like to sit?"

Beth glanced around. "Not by a window. Let me order my lunch since this isn't a date." She regarded him.

"Okay."

She waited in line behind him. "So, when did you become a Christian?"

"Since I was fifteen."

"And how old are you now?" She asked.

"I can help whoever is next," a woman behind another register announced.

Stan walked over to the next line and ordered an Asian salad. Did Beth enjoy salads? He guessed, by looking at her, that she never ate healthy. He hoped he would be a good influence on her. He scratched his head, wondering why he would be interested in her.

Remember, you were once overweight. Just be the friend she needs.

"Yes, Lord." After he paid for his lunch, he headed for a table toward the center of the room. He couldn't wait to know Beth as friends. She stated she had an on-and-off relationship with Jesus. She piqued his interest and his pulse increased.

****

Saved by the bell. Not that he wanted to keep his age from her, but she giggled. Stan was nice, but he wasn't her type. She rubbed her head, thinking about her mother. Ann liked Stan. She had high hopes their friendship could lead to dating. She was in her early thirties and her mother was concerned Beth would never marry if she didn't lose weight. The two of them talking at the gym excited her mother. It annoyed her.

Stan walked toward the dining area as she ordered a taco salad with a large diet Coke. What if she didn't lose weight? Would he still want her? Men would marry overweight women because the women usually wouldn't divorce them. Was Stan that way? She scolded herself for thinking more than friendship.

"Your order number is 39."

"Thanks." She walked toward Stan, who kept his eye on her.

"I'm thirty," he said, answering her question. "And you?"

"Don't you have a cell phone with Facebook or something?"

He chuckled. "I'm old-fashioned. If I am with a lady, I don't want to be rude."

"Why not? Everyone does it." She sat in the chair.

"I am not everyone. I'm more interested in my friend here than Facebook."

Her stomach quivered, and she shook her head. "Yeah, right."

Stan smiled as he gazed at her. "I mean it, Beth. I am."

"Number 38, your order is ready."

Beth relaxed. She had wanted to bolt, and nausea overcame her. Oh, God! This is going to become a date! I'm not ready! And am I going to see him Monday at the gym? Was there somewhere she could hide? She glanced around. Seeing her car helped her to relax. She could leave now…No, she couldn't. Lunch was going to be long.

Stan returned to his seat and smiled. He removed the top and tore open the salad dressing.

She took a quick breath. "Thirty-one."

"Huh? Oh. I will be thirty-one in August."

Her heart raced as she widened her eyes. "What? Really? What day?"

"Eighth."

She relaxed. Good. We're not born on the same day. "Mine is the twenty-first."

He gave her a dazed look. "Of August?"

She nodded, not looking at him.

"Well, we got something in common—besides being Christians."

"You don't wait for me." She stared at his salad.

"I want to. Are you uncomfortable around me?"

"You can tell?"

"Yes. I don't have hidden agendas. I want to know you as friends."

Her mother's words rang in her head. "Sometimes friendship leads to dating." She glanced around, then at herself. She wasn't ready for a relationship. And was this dating to him? She shouldn't have accepted. She couldn't wait to move out and have a place of her own. Since she quit her job at another book store years ago, she had loss of income and couldn't pay rent anymore. After she gained weight, she lost confidence in herself and moved in with her parents.

"Number 39, your order is ready."

Beth excused herself and rose to her feet. She ambled to the front

*****

He sensed her insecurity. He understood. He was in her place before. “Dear, Lord, help me to show my genuine interest in her.”

Before she can accept your compliments, she must accept herself.

“If I didn’t know better, I think she wanted to leave.” He understood. He met a beautiful woman prior to losing weight. She was a Christian, but he blew her off with his insecurities. No, I won’t be blown off. I’ll be patient. If she didn’t want to talk, fine.

Give her time and she will confide in you.

“Yes, God.”

He smiled as Beth returned to the table. He would keep his word.

****

The room became quiet except for a few people talking in the background. Over to her right, people were snickering at her. They’re laughing at me.

“Are you okay?”

“I’m…fine.”

He nodded and continued eating.

Stan hadn’t said anything more. Was he judging me? Maybe he was being nice and feeling sorry for me. Why was he not asking her any more questions?

Something dropped in the kitchen and she jumped. Nerves. She tried calming them. “Spit it out!”

“Spit what out? My food?”

"You're ugly. I'm used to it."

"I have none. I wished there was something I could say to help you relax."

"Really?"

He stared at her. "I see you how Jesus sees you."

"And how does Jesus see me?"

"Beautiful."

"You…see me…as beautiful? You're not feeling sorry for me?"

"Not at all."

She exhaled. "I'm sorry I'm a nervous wreck."

"Do you act this way around your other friends?"

"No. They're females. One lives on a farm and the other on a ranch on Montana. Holly was the only local friend who didn't want her way after–" She bit her tongue before she discussed her abuse. She wasn't ready to share that part of her life.

"After?" He munched on lettuce.

"I strayed."

"From?"

"My faith." She stared out the window

"Why did you go astray?"

"Not ready to tell you. I'm done." She put her fork down. She lost her appetite.

"You hardly touched your salad."

"I'm not hungry anymore. I'll take it home." She covered her salad.

"I'm sorry if I ruined your lunch."

"I had a bad date before I met you. It was probably not a good idea to have lunch with you, but I wanted to make my mom happy." She picked up her salad and ran out the door

Four

"How was your lunch?" Beth tried to sneak in, not looking at her mother. "What happened?" She followed Beth to her room.

"Nothing." She lied. "We ate lunch."

"You mean he ate lunch? Yours is in your hand."

"Mom, I don't want to talk discuss my lunch." She sat on her bed.

"Did he reject you?"

"No! I…rejected him."

"What? Why? He is a nice guy!"

Beth shot her mom a look. "How would you know? Mother's instinct?"

"Yes. Is he a Christian?"

"Yes. Mom, we just had lunch as friends, but it felt more like a date and I panicked. I hope I don't see him again."

Ann gasped. "You can't mean that."

"I told you I'm not into dating."

"He didn't ask you out. Why are you worried?"

"Because I remember what you said."

"What did I say?"

"Friendship leads to something else."

"Oh." She joined her on the bed. "I'm sorry, sweetheart. Listen, you're a grown woman. If you don't want to see him again, then don't." She sighed.

"Thanks, mom. Maybe after a month."

In a month, if she works hard. She could lose a couple of inches, but not her level of confidence, which wasn't high enough to date him. He didn't attract her. But he wanted to be friends. Did she have to attract him to be friends? Something he said struck her. Beautiful? How could he say that to her? She didn't feel beautiful.

"What exactly did happen?" her mother broke the silence.

"I panicked when he asked me why I drifted."

"He is showing interest."

"As a friend?"

"Yes. Beth, you need friends. Whatever happen to the ones you had?

"Julie lives in Montana and Holly is busy on her father's farm. The rest deserted me."

"Are you positive? Friends should love at all times, not when it's easy."

Beth rose to her feet and walked to her window. "I'm a loser to them. I'm fat and ugly."

"Stop feeling sorry for yourself. Working out is the first step. Eating healthy is the next step."

A few tears fell. "I'm trying not to feel sorry for myself."

Two people holding hands walked past their house. An ache rose up in her chest. Deep inside, she wanted a man in her life. Someone who would love her unconditionally and as she is.

There is.

Who?

Stan.

"No!"

"No what?" Her mother put a hand on her shoulders.

Stan had a friend with him. What was he like? Was he available? Maybe she'll pay more attention next time. Maybe she'll flirt with him if she dared.

Who are you kidding? You'd think he'll be interested in you? You're better off alone.

"Shut up!"

"Me?"

"No. I need to be alone, mom."

"Are we on for Scrabble later?"

"As long as we don't discuss my lack of a love life."

"We won't. I promise."

A weak smile formed on her face. "Okay."

****

Larry was watching a boxing match on ESPN when Stan entered his apartment. "How was your lunch? Does she want to see you again?"

Touching the base of his neck, he replied, "Well, she definitely thought I was a jerk. Somehow I had turned her off." He plopped down in the couch.

"Ahh, man! I'm sorry. What happened?" He turned the TV off and reclined with Stan.

"I guess I got too personal with her. I haven't dated in a while–"

“I thought you were going out as friends.”

Stan scratched his heads. “We were, but my questions made her uncomfortable.”

“Do you still like her?”

“Not sure. She is nice, but I don’t think I’m her type.”

“You don’t have to be anyone’s type to have friends.”

“Then why would she give me that impression?”

“I don’t know. Ask God.”

“I might do that. I have plenty of time.”

“Don’t forget. We have a bachelor party to go to. Daryl’s getting married.”

“Six p.m. I know.” He smiled.

Stan pushed himself up from the old beat-up couch. Living a bachelor life had suited him, but a desire in his heart had called him to seek a woman for his life. His lunch with Beth went south. He listened to his friend and now to God. Wouldn’t God had given him success? Instead the woman rejected him. She barely ate her salad.

“God, I never had women friends. How do I treat her as a friend and not a girlfriend?” He chuckled. Beth was both a female and a friend, but people these days gave boyfriends and girlfriends new meaning. They saw them as a date. Did Beth flee because he had treated their lunch as a date?

During his time of prayer, he sensed Beth may be interested in his friend. Larry was not committed to any woman but has female friends. Would Larry be interested in her?

Five

Stan woke up at the crack of dawn. The house was still dark. He put on his robe and grabbed his Bible. The black leather-bound Bible was a gift from his grandmother before she passed away.

"I want you to pray and ask God for guidance before reading it. He will give you light for every situation you are in."

He had forgotten those precious words until he was at rock bottom five years ago. Although a Christian, he had failed. He resorted to alcohol to forget his problems until he met Larry at the church he attended. If Larry hadn't offered to share his apartment with him, he would have ended up on the streets, jobless.

Now at thirty, his life was back on track, but he needed a woman who loved God as much as he did. He read a book called "Praying for Your Future Wife." Beth wasn't his type, but if God had other plans, He would have to show him.

"Lord, I perceive that Beth isn't interested in me, even as friends. How can I change that?" He regarded Larry. His friend and roommate had a good head of wavy brown hair and never had a problem with weight.

Pray for her.

"Anything particular?"

It is not you, but herself. She has insecurities. If you allow the Holy Spirit to direct your prayers, you'll do fine.

So, Stanley prayed, using his prayer language.

****

"Rise and shine, sweetheart! Today is Sunday!" Beth's mom flipped on the light and Beth's head throbbed.

"I'm up, mom." She rubbed her head and then uncovered herself. "Last night Larry was in my dream"

"What happened in your dream?'

"He appeared to me as an angel."

"With wings?"

Beth reached for her robe, which was at the end of her bed, and slipped it on. "I didn't see any."

"How did you know he was an angel?" She led her daughter to their kitchen.

"His face was shiny, and he had an ethereal appearance."

"Okay."

"I might like him."

"Because he was in your dream?"

"Maybe. Stan gives me the impression he wants to control me."

"Yeah, right."

Jason greeted folks as he walked in, and Ann kept her eyes off him. "Good morning, ladies," he said, reaching their pew.

"Good morning, Jason," Ann responded. "Care to join us?"

Jason walked in alone. His wife of seven years died of breast cancer and he had one child to care for alone. His daughter was in the second-grade class. "The McKnights invited me, but thanks for the offer." He noted Beth. "Beth, how are you?"

"Good," she responded, and he walked on by.

"See? He isn't interested in me. We are friends."

"So, you asked him that to show me?"

Her mother sighed. "Well, partially, yes. I figured he wouldn't join us." She gave her a weak smile. Her mother was hurt by his rejection.

"Oh, mom."

"I'm fine."

"Maybe the attraction will grow."

Her mother sat up as if she realized something. "But I wasn't looking for him."

"Whatever."

"I do hope you give Stan a chance."

"I'll think about it."

"Pray too." She smiled. She took her worship guide and hid her face behind it.

Beth knew Jason's rejection hurt her mother. Ann was brave. Maybe Jesus was telling them it wasn't the right time. Three months was a short time. "There is a book out by Kathy Broccoli and Dee Brestin. Maybe we could use the study guide."

"Beth, I am in love with Jesus. I will always be."

A headache threatened to invade her mind as she rubbed her temples. Why couldn't her mom leave her alone if her mom was happy not dating? Did she want to date? No, she realized her mom wanted Beth to have a life. Her only daughter, who had been her best friend since she returned to California. Shouldn't her mom have a life? Her mother was more interested in finding a man for her daughter than having one herself. Beth could find a man for herself. Not until I feel good about my body.

Jason sat two rows in front of them, by two older couple who were the McKnights. Jason was closer to her age than her mom's. At least he looked young, in his thirties.

Your mom isn't interested in dating Jason. She is interested in hooking you up with him.

"Mom, how old is Jason? He has a seven-year-old."

"Thirty-nine. Why?"

"He's a little too young for you, isn't he?"

"He's not old enough to be my son." She smiled. "Besides, I told you he isn't interested in me and we're just friends."

Stan wanted friendship too. Or did he feel sorry for her? Stan might have helped and encouraged her, but he couldn't be in the weight room with her. Was she too picky? Beth returned her attention to Jason.

Before she could daydream, the associate pastor spoke as he welcomed everyone.

Stan drove his car to Sunnyvale Community Bible Church. The same church where he met Larry, a divorced man of four years. Divorce was common in the church. Members justified divorce when it came to unfaithfulness. As for Larry, he had married too young and after a year of marriage, his wife left him for another man. He had told Stan he was happy being a bachelor.

A Man For Beth

Larry parked his green Ford Prius next to Stan's Volvo. Larry could have Beth if he wanted her. Didn't she catch him staring at her? When Larry stepped out, Stan asked, "Do you like Beth?"

"I don't know. I try not to judge by appearance. Why?"

"Maybe her type?"

"You're not giving Beth a chance." He followed Stan to the sanctuary.

"I did. I think she'd rather not be friends."

"Pal, she's scared."

A couple of older female greeters gave Stan and Larry a worship guide.

"I dreamt she kissed you." Stan said.

"What?" His face reddened. "Dreams are work of fiction."

"So? You deny you're not interested in her?"

"I deny nothing. I'm not into dating. Bachelor life suits me just fine."

Stan couldn't keep from smiling. Larry could use a woman. The two of them reminded him of a classic TV show called the Odd Couple. Stan was a neat freak while Larry was sloppy. Often, he had to pick up after his roommate. He wondered if Larry was sloppy when he was married. His wife would pick up after him. Larry never told him why Bernice left him.

"You think I'm looking for a woman?" Stan asked as they sat in a pew behind a family of four. The two young kids, ages 3 and 5, stared at them and Stan made a funny face. The kids giggled.

"Why are you two kids giggling?" Their mother glanced at Stan who kept a straight face, but Larry laughed at his attempt.

"You're a class act. I bet Beth would love your sense of humor." Larry challenged him.

"Didn't we teach you it's not polite to stare?" The mother told her children.

"But mom-"

"No, buts." She offered an apologetic smile. "Sorry about that, Stan."

"No worries. I was a precocious five-year-old once." He winked at the five-year-old, but the kid had turned around. The worship had ended, and as the ushers had passed around the collection plate, the pastor stepped up to the pulpit. "The title of the sermon is called When God Won't Calm your Storms. Please turn to Matthew eight verse twenty-three as our text for the day

After the service, the congregation members rose from their seats and mingled a little while with others, but Stan and Larry ambled out toward the lobby area.

"Hello, Larry." A woman with reddish blonde hair and sporting thin-framed glasses approached him. She grabbed his hand, but he pulled away.

"What do you want, Bernice?" He crossed his arms.

She pursed her lip as if the words wouldn't come out. "A second chance?" She offered a faint smile.

He folded his arms. "Let me guess. Your new love left you?"

"I'll be going. See you at the apartment." Stan walked toward the door

"It won' be long," Larry said.

Stan exited the lobby and walked to his car.! He never had seen her until now and she was beautiful, but he hoped Larry could discern her motives. Larry told him he enjoyed being a bachelor; he'll brush her off.

"Told you," Larry said, catching up to Stan.

Stan grinned. "You didn't give her a second chance."

"She isn't a Christian. I questioned her motive for coming to church. God told me they weren't pure."

Stan chuckled. Larry was wise and discerning. "She sought you??"

"Her boyfriend dumped her for another woman."

Stan felt a tickle in his ribs, but he suppressed the urge to laugh. "I'm glad you listened to the Lord. Maybe you will think–"

"Don't mention Beth. I told you–"

"Larry, she may be interested in you. You don't know unless you ask her on a date."

"No!"

****

The sermon was what Beth needed to hear. Her heart pounded when the pastor spoke about Identity in Christ. She had such low self-esteem and because of her experiences with men, she had trust issues. Because of her trust issues, she had difficulty accepting friendship with men. She forgot who she was in Christ. "Accepted in the beloved." Her cheeks radiated. "If God accepts me as I am, I should accept myself."

"Yes, you should. You were wonderfully and fearfully created in my womb." Her mother beamed.

"I need time with myself after lunch. Do you mind?"

"No."

"I would love to spend time with Jesus, my first love."

"I am glad you took something away from the sermon."

"Would you like go out for lunch with me? I'm hungry for pizza."

"Pizza on a Sunday? We can go to A Fresh Start. We can have a salad."

She wrinkled her nose. Her mother wanted to help her eat healthy, but would having pizza hurt her diet? She held her stomach as if she would vomit. "A salad?"

"Have you been to A Fresh Start?"

"No, but–"

"Then don't judge until you try."

She moaned. "Fine. A Fresh Start it is."

"Now is a good time to start eating healthy."

"Okay. Mother. Okay!" She was exasperated. Here she was at thirty years of age and her mother was still trying to dictate her life. On the other hand, she appreciated her mom helping her to lose weight; she put on a brave face.

Six

As the waitress seated them at A Fresh Start, her mother had a faraway look in her eyes and a smile on her face. "What's on your mind, mom?" The waitress handed Beth the menu and she thanked her.

"Wouldn't it be something if Stan and his friend came in?"

Beth hoped not. Her mother liked him, but Stan didn't interest her. Only his friend appealed to her. She wouldn't mind seeing his friend. *I'll have to ask him his name.*

The bell on the door jingled. Beth didn't have to look when her mother's mouth dropped open. "No." Beth groaned.

And her mother did the unthinkable. She waved over to them. "Hi, guys!"

A tingle swept across her neck and her chest tightened as she hid herself in the menu. *Oh God, when will this end?*

"Stan, why you don't you join us?"

"We don't want to interrupt you time together, but it's nice to see Beth eating here. Nice to see you, Beth."

Beth peeked at Larry. His smile swept her off her feet. "You too."

"Do you come here every Sunday?" Ann asked.

"Excuse me, but I need to use the lady's room. If the waitress returns, please order for me." Beth jumped out of her seat and rushed past Stan to the bathroom.

Her stomach rumbled, and she thought she would heave. Beth needed to calm down but couldn't. Her mother embarrassed her. "I need to move out."

"Are you all right, miss?" An older woman asked.

"I…think so. I just have a bad case of nerves."

"I hope you'll be okay. Do you need anything?"

Beth stared at her flushed face in the mirror. "Do you have children?" The woman looked to be in her late fifties. She might have grand babies

"I have two. They are both in college right now."

She turned her attention to the woman. "And your husband?"

The woman sighed. "Is working."

"I'm sorry. My name is Beth." She offered her hand.

"Dorothy. Are you here alone?"

"I'm with my mom."

"That's sweet; I wish I had my mom. She died when I was twelve."

Beth didn't know what to say. She complained her mother embarrassed her and here was a woman who was motherless for 40 plus years. "Who…who did you live with? Your father?"

"My aunt. My mother took care of me as a single parent until she died of leukemia at the age of 32."

"She was young!"

"I know, but I am grateful." She gave a warm smile. "I had two best friends who were the world for me and my aunt took me to church, where I accepted Jesus in my heart. Are you a Christian?"

"Yes. I was the lost sheep Jesus looked for

"Aww, well bless your soul. I should let you go."

"Thanks." Beth exited the restroom, feeling better. Her limbs tingled, and knees went weak. "Thank you!" She felt overwhelmed by the blessing God had bestowed on her. Dorothy had no parents, but she had her mom. Tears poured from her eyes.

Stan and Larry were gone as she arrived back. Her tension left her body. She sat and reached for her mom's hand. "I love you. Sorry if I haven't told you."

"Did you have an encounter with Jesus?"

"Sort of. But he used an older woman."

"I love you too, sweetie. I want you to be happy. I'm sorry if I'm pushing Stan on you."

"What happened while I was away?"

The waitress returned with an order pad. "Ready to order?"

"Yes! I'll have the garden salad with lemon vinaigrette." Ann said happily.

"Umm," Beth glanced at the menu. She wasn't a salad person. Would a salad do? She glanced at her mother. No. Ann was paying for lunch. She would have to stick to a salad. "Strawberry Mandarin looks interesting. Balsamic vinaigrette. To drink, I will have a diet Coke."

"Water for me."

The waitress finished writing their orders, then walked back to the kitchen.

"To answer your question, they went to their table. They come here every Sunday and I asked Larry a hypothetical question. You can forget him."

Beth gasped. "What? You asked?"

"I asked if he has a girlfriend. I didn't mention your name."

"He might have assumed you were setting me up with him."

"Would you have asked him?"

"I don't know if I would have or not."

"Stan isn't much into dating either. I think he only wants friendship." She took a drink of her water.

"I want neither. I prefer female friends."

Her mom didn't respond.

****

Beth ran like she had an emergency. Was she sick? "Is she feeling okay?" Stan asked.

"Just a bad case of nerves. She'll be fine. I have a question. Does Larry have a girlfriend?"

Earlier he suggested Larry was not interested in dating, but Larry brushed off the suggestion. "I doubt she is interested in me."

"If she asked?"

"Yes, I will."

Larry had a thick head of hair compared to him. Larry attracted her. He would be happy to let Larry date her. He hasn't seen him with a woman. One time, as they walked to a gym, a member asked if they were gay, but she didn't offend him. He told the member they were bachelors. Stan smiled to Larry.

"No, but I'm not interested in dating"

"He is a confirmed bachelor."

"Were you married?"

"Once."

"What about you, Stan? You took interest in my daughter."

"I like her, but I doubt she is interested in me.

Ann took a drink of water. "She came out of a couple bad experiences. Give her time."

"Bad experiences?" They both had that in common. He could help her.

She doesn't want your help.

"I probably shouldn't tell you." She said.

"How was your church service?"

"The service was good. Are you going to the gym tomorrow night or morning?"

He cleared his throat. As he was going to tell her, a waitress led them to a table. So much for that.

The men followed the waitress and waited to be seated. Both scanned the menu, but Stan spoke first. "Did you notice how Beth ran right after we arrived?"

Larry ignored the question. "Did you think the Lord led Beth and her mom here today?"

"I hope he did. I'd like to stay in is will"

They had always ordered the same salad, but Stan wanted a sandwich for a change. A Panini sounded good. What did Beth order? Beth hadn't eaten here, especially on Sundays. What church did she attend? When he caught a glimpse of her, her natural beauty shined forth. He wished Beth wouldn't run from him. *Why did she run, Lord?* He would pray.

"I think I will have the chicken Caesar salad. "What about you?"

****

They were home. Beth followed her mother into the house and dashed upstairs to her room. After her experience in the bathroom, she wanted to spend time with Jesus. She put into practice ACTS, which stands for adoration, confession, thanksgiving and supplication. "You are the joy of my desire. The apple of my eye. You are my rock and my fortress. God, I need You more than ever…" On and on she went as she adored him and worshiped Him. "Lord, is there sin in my life?" She waited for Him. She knew she wasn't perfect, but He had forgiven in the past. She tried her best to live for Him. "Lord, did you send Stan my way?" Did Stan know she'd be there or did her mother call him and invite him to join them? Her mother didn't have his number? If she called him, she could have looked up his number. And the faraway look as if she was planning something. She pushed aside her questions. "I should trust mom. Lord, I know she is trying to help, but she is forcing him on me."

How do you know that?

Huh? An answer! Her face reddened. "Know what, God?"

That she is forcing him on you? Have you thought your mother is asking me to help her find a man for you?

"Did she? What was your answer?"

Trust me.

"I'm going to be honest here. I don't like Stan. I don't feel attracted to him."

Stan just wants your friendship. He knows you're not ready to date.

"I prefer female friends."

****

Stan and Larry didn't plan on meeting Beth and her mother at A Fresh Start. Neither of them recalled them dining there before that day. It had to be God's idea for them to meet, but Beth didn't seem happy. Why did she run to the bathroom so fast? He admired their relationship. Beth cared for her daughter and they were close. When Beth was in the ladies' room, Ann told him about her relationship with their daughter. She was widowed, and they have been close since Beth moved back home. Ann shared that her husband died five years ago. Stan grew up with an abusive father. He admired the relationship she had with her mother. He wasn't jealous. How old was Beth when her father passed? While Stan's father was alive, he lived with his stepmother, with whom he bonded when he was a teen. She was a godly woman who didn't fear his father. Did Beth have a good relationship with her father?

"Penny for your thoughts." Larry plopped down on the couch next to him.

Stan regarded him. "You know I was 18 and doing drugs and alcohol."

"Yes. You told me."

"My stepmother prayed I would get help. I did." He smiled at Larry. "I think Ann is trying to help her daughter the same way Eloise helped me. I admire that."

"So, Beth is on your mind?"

"Her relationship with her mother. I'm going to give Beth time. It had to be God's plan for us to meet the ladies at A Fresh Start."

"I agree."

"I like Beth as a friend."

"Just be patient."

"I will." He used the remote control to turn on a baseball game.

Seven

The next five days, Beth felt herself relaxing, as she had had no recent encounters with Stan. Every tension in her body melted away as she rang up customer purchases. Stan wouldn't be a customer since he worked at the other book store.

The other bookstore. Beth smiled. How was it that they both love books? And the coincidence at A Fresh Start? Did her mother secretly ask Stan to meet them at A Fresh Start? Her face reddened. She was sure her mother did. Her mother managed her both times! What must he think of her? *I'm 30 years old and I live with my mom! Stan probably lives in a messy apartment, enjoying bachelor life. Does Larry live with him?*

Larry was another story. Tall and handsome with his dark brown wavy hair and brown eyes. Her heart fluttered, but God reminded her that he wasn't interested in her and her heart dropped into her stomach. Beth frowned.

"You have a customer, Beth." Jamie, her employer brought her out of her introspection.

"Huh? Oh." She turned her attention to a female customer waiting to purchase her book. Beth took the scanner and scanned the bar code. "$24.74."

The woman took her checkbook out and wrote a check.

"May I see your ID?"

She removed a card and showed her.

Beth gasped. The woman's birthday showed she was 46, but the woman looked twentyish! How was that possible?

Denise smiled. “Cosmetic surgery. I get that reaction all the time.”

Beth proceeded with authorizing the check and she returned a smile. “You have children?”

“Two. Both in college.”

“I bet people mistake them for your siblings.”

“Yes, they do.”

“Anything else you need?”

“No, this is it and thanks for the compliment…Beth.” She read her name tag. “My daughter’s name is Elizabeth after the woman in the Bible.”

“You read the Bible? I’m a Christian too.”

“I could tell by the light in your eyes. Well, nice to meet you.”

“Likewise.”

Denise took her book and left.

Denise reminded her of someone. The lady wasn’t old enough to be her mother. Had she seen her somewhere before? She examined the check. “Brian and Denise Jones.” Her heart raced and her skin tingled. Could this be the author of Deadly Impact? She read that book twice since she ordered the book two years ago. Did she have an encounter with an author? And in this small town of 25,000? “Jamie, was she–”

“Denise Jones the author? Yes.” She said it in a matter-of-fact manner. Must have been no surprise to her employer. “Had she come here before?”

“We sell all her books. She had a book signing here when Deadly Impact came out. Quite a turnout.” A book signing. A small reminder of what would have happened to her a few months ago if she hadn't flirted with Brad, aka Drew. She shuddered every time she thought of him. *I wonder if Julie reads Denise's books.* From what she'd seen, Julie read charismatic books like the one by Sally Parker, who wrote Deep Calls onto Deep. Beth smiled. Thank you, Lord, for the opportunity to see an author face to face.

*****

The bells on the door chimed as customers entered and exited the bookstore. He climbed up the rolling ladder to shelve books. The book in his hand was on breaking addiction. Not long ago he was addicted to cocaine. Larry helped him break out of his addiction and told him about Jesus. His self-esteem was at an all-time low. He had dated women who had used him and discarded him, but Jesus took him out of the dump they threw him in. The song Everything was his life song. He identified with the man Jesus wooed into a relationship. He wanted what the world had to offer, but what the world offered left him empty.

Beth. Was she the same way? From his experiences, his weight gave him low self-esteem. He wanted to help her. And if she wasn't interested in him, fine.

"How are you doing there, Stan?" his supervisor asked.

"Getting the last book shelved." He scanned the book. Somewhere deep inside, something told him her addiction was sweets. I bet she was once a beautiful thin woman.

Are you shallow?

"Stan?"

"Sorry." His face reddened.

"Stan, are you in love? You're blushing!"

"Not exactly in love but thinking." He smiled.

"Take her on a date. What's she like?"

"It's not for me to say. She's in a fragile place."

"But you like her?"

"Yes, I do."

"I hope it works out for you. When you're done, I have another job for you."

"Okay."

She walked toward her office.

He hoped so too. He wanted a friendship with her. If God sent her his way for more than friendship, He would have to orchestrate it. A peace washed over him concerning her. He took in slow and steady breaths. "Your will be done."

Stan stepped down the ladder and headed over to his manager's office. "You have an assignment?"

Lora looked his way from her computer screen and smiled at Stan. "I need you to watch the store while I run an errand."

Watching the store was not in his job description, though he had worked there for years. His eyes widened. "You want me to watch the store? What happened to Mitchel?" Mitchel had worked longer than Stan. He worked as the cashier while he shelved books.

"He's on lunch break."

Was it noon already? He checked his watch. "11:30."

"Yes. He breaks at noon, and then you break."

"You need me behind the cash register?" He hoped.

"Lisa is behind the register."

He chuckled. “What you want me to do? Stand as a sentry?”

“You’re cute, Stan. No, I’m asking you to supervise. Make sure everyone is on the up and up.”

“There isn’t anything for me to do?”

“Not now.” She closed her laptop and he watched her tall lean body bend over her desk as her luscious hair swung around her delicate neck. Lora could have anyone she wanted, but she settled for an accountant three inches shorter than her. She must like short men, he mused. Stan stood the same height as Lisa, but he had muscles to add to his weight.

“I’ll watch the store.”

“Great!” She led Stan out of her office and walked to the cashier. “Lisa, Stan will be supervising for a while. I have an errand to run.”

“Sure, Lora.” She eyed Stan but looked down. Was he attracted to her? They had worked together since Lora hired her two years ago, taking the place of a former employee who had moved to Los Angeles to try for an acting job. He liked Lisa, but he didn’t want to give her an impression she interested him. The Lord told him not to date women based on appearance. And Lisa was eye catching.

Stan kept his eye on the store. There was no need, but Lora was his employer. He never complained either. Scripture taught him to do everything without complaining. He whistled and greeted people as they came in.

Shortly before noon, Lora returned. “Go ahead and take your lunch break.”

Stan took out his cell phone as he exited the store.

Eight

"Ready to go to the gym?" Beth's mother asked, poking her head in Beth's room.

Beth felt a heaviness in her chest. She didn't want to. The last time was too hard, and her mother embarrassed her. She didn't want to run into Stan. She survived the workdays without seeing him. "No."

"We leave in ten minutes."

Why did she have to listen to her mom? She couldn't wait to have money and save up to leave home. The money she had years ago was spent. Her ex-boyfriend told her she should trust God and give her money to him through a ministry. She did, and she ended up broke except for the meager amount of money she had for fuel.

But she did want to get her life back.

Somewhere deep inside, she wanted someone to love her and accept her.

There's Stan.

Beth stopped in mid-step. Stan? She struggled with accepting him in her life. She couldn't get past her mother setting her up with him. Or did God set her up? Did God want Stan in her life?

It was time to seek God. Her Bible laid on her bedside stand. *I have been reading the Bible. Just haven't spent enough time as I used to.*

"Beth?" Her mother appeared in her room. "Ready?"

"Can we leave a little later?"

Her mother's mouth dropped open. "Why?"

"I need to spend time with Jesus to prepare for what is ahead."

Ann checked the time on her watch. "I guess we can leave a half hour later. Enjoy your time with Jesus." She exited her room, but Beth detected disappointment from her mother.

"Lord, if you are going to bring a man into my life, bring one into hers too." How long has her mother been without one? Wasn't it time for her mother to live life apart from her?

"Jesus, why does Stan like me? I mean I know he wants to be friends. But I prefer his friend. Could he set me up with Larry?"

She waited. She opened her Bible, hoping the Holy Spirit would lead her to a verse. Julie said He does. She would wait.

And she found herself reading Proverbs 31:10 "Who can find a virtuous wife? For her worth is far more than rubies."

"Hmm. Virtuous. Am I virtuous to him?" She rolled the question around in her head.

"Are you ready?"

She shifted her attention to above her and smiled. "Well, here goes." She closed her Bible and headed out her room, carrying her duffel bag. "I guess I am now."

On the way there, Beth asked, "Am I virtuous?"

"I heard you reading Proverbs 31. Good chapter."

"God led me there."

"Do you know what the premise of that section of the chapter is about? When I was in college, before I met your dad, I was in a women's Bible study group. They spent an entire month on Proverbs 31, but they read from the NLT."

"The New Living Translation?"

"Yes. I've memorized verse ten because I reminded myself if I wanted a husband I needed to be virtuous."

"And?"

"He wasn't looking for a virtuous woman. Your dad and I were friends first and I didn't see him as anything else. I didn't care for his job and the money he made was not worth taking care of the family, so I kept my options open.

At one point during our friendship time, he wanted to read the Bible as a couple. The idea scared me. He saw me as his girlfriend."

"Where did you read from?"

"Ephesians."

Beth's eyes widened. "Why did he choose Ephesians?"

"I discovered he was a man of prayer. He wanted a woman of prayer, so I went along, but I was still scared."

"Dad wasn't your type?"

"Hardly, but God had to open my eyes. I prayed one night and the same night, I dreamt we were in a spiritual battle. I never get prophetic dreams and this dream scared me. It was when I realized he was more than what I needed. I had to look past those superficial things and see his heart. Your dad knew I wasn't interested in him, but he was in me."

Her heart seemed to pound, then freeze. She was simply at a loss for words. Had she fallen into her mom's path? Beth wouldn't be alive today if they hadn't met, if her mom hadn't listened to the Lord. Yet something her mother said increased her pulse. "What did dad do?"

Ann's mouth wrinkled at the corners as she smiled. "He flipped burgers at Burger Basket."

"Full time? Or part time? Is that how you met him?"

"Yes. My girlfriend Sylvia and I had lunch there one Saturday and we were in line. When we were closer to the front, he was smiling at me. Sylvia whispered. 'I think he likes you.' As for your question, full time."

"What did you want in a husband?"

Ann giggled. "I wanted to marry my college professor. He was quite a catch for any lucky woman and he was single. He taught my favorite subject, which was English Literature. I got an A in his class."

"And he wasn't interested in you?"

"The good Lord knew my motives weren't pure and he knew that before I could have a relationship, I needed to grow in mine with Him. So, I cultivated my relationship with the Lord and that was why I agreed to attend Bible study with my man.

Six months later, your dad asked me out on a date."

Did her mom make this up to encourage her to give Stan a try? Could she doubt her mom? All the years she lived with her mother, her mom was nothing like Julie. No, her faith was more like Julie's husband—a baby Christian. "Why didn't I see you reading the Bible or hear you pray?"

Her mother sighed, and a tear fell down her face. "I kind of fell away. After your father died, I blamed God, like most people do in those situations. I isolated myself. When I heard you moved in with a man, my heart broke. I wondered if I failed you–"

"But when dad was alive, I don't remember you two reading the Bible or praying."

"Sweetheart, we did. We did these things in private."

"You weren't showing Christ too much to me."

"I'm sorry, sweetheart. Your father left that to me to do and I didn't want to interfere in your life. Maybe if I had, you wouldn't have joined a cult. I blame myself."

"Don't blame yourself, Mom."

"I was too much of an enabler."

*****

Stan spent thirty minutes in prayer before he and Larry took off to the gym. The last verse he read stayed in his mind. "Be completely humble and patient, bearing one another in love."

Larry walked in. "What are you reading?" He put his foot on the bed and leaned toward Stan. "The book of Ephesians. The Lord instructed me to be patient with her."

"In accepting your friendship."

"And gentle, yes." He smiled.

"You would have to be gentle with a woman...especially if they victims of abuse."

"Yeah, I get that from her. She doesn't like discussing it."

"Women are all touchy and emotional. Talk about yourself to her. That way, she won't get upset for asking a personal question."

"I can do that."

"And let her share when she is ready."

"Why do you know so much about women? You haven't gotten one for yourself." He ribbed his friend, laughing

"Just because I'm not interested doesn't mean I'm clueless. I have a sister, you know."

Stan closed his Bible and grabbed his gym bag. "Well, let's hit the gym!"

"Think Beth will be there?" He followed Stan out to their cars, toting his gym bag.

"If she is, she'll be gawking at you." Stan continued with the ribbing. Both have been friends long enough not to let a little teasing hurt or offend them. It was in good fun.

"Ha-ha." Larry climbed into his car before Stan disappeared in his.

Stan chuckled. It would work with Larry and Beth. Could he set his friend up with Beth or did the Lord have plans for him and Beth? What Larry said went through his mind. *Women are all touchy and emotional.* Beth wasn't that way, was she?. "Lord, either you help me set him up with Beth–"

What makes you think I will help you set your friend up? Have you thought that I am helping Larry with you?

"But God, she gives me the impression she is not interested in me."

Not yet. Give her time.

Then there was the scripture that lingered in his mind. Patience, humility and gentleness wrapped in those last three words. He had to ask. “The scripture I read today - was that for me? You want me to be gentle and patient with her?”

Yes.

A glimmer of hope stirred in his heart and a smile broke out in his face. “Yes, Lord.”

Larry followed him. He hadn’t realized that until Larry parked his car behind a cute little bug. For some reason, it reminded him of Beth. Once she gets her weight down, she could drive a VW bug.

Patience and gentle.

“I got you, Lord.” He smiled as he pointed to heaven. He followed Larry into the gym.

Two women walked away from the front desk and heading toward the locker room. His heart soared at recognizing Beth.

“Lord, this has to be your doing.” He grinned.

Beth glanced his way and his pulse raced. He gave her a little smile. “We didn’t follow you.”

She turned back and whispered to her mother, then glanced back, smiling this time.

Larry grinned. “She is warning up to you. Your turn to sign in.”

“I’m ready.” He showed his membership card to the lady behind the counter, then followed Larry to the locker room.

Nine

After the workout, Beth and her mother showered to cool off and wash the sweat off. It was a good workout and Beth felt reinvigorated. "I'm glad we went tonight." Beth dried herself.

"Even though you saw Stan?"

"It was bound to happen. If you didn't insist I come, I would have not."

Her mother offered a huge smile. "In a month, you'll start to feel better. Did you weigh yourself today?"

"Lost a pound."

"Keep it up."

"Thanks for your encouragement." She planted a kiss on her mom's cheek. "What are mothers for?" She returned her kiss. "I love you."

"Love you too, mom." She felt warm and fuzzy. She imagined her mom seeing a warm glow on her face.

"I think the workout has brought us closer together."

She disagreed. There were other ways to bring them closer together. They connected because of their relationship with men. A question surfaced in her mind. "Were you ever fat?"

A tear fell. "Yes, but not from overeating. I didn't eat to feel better, but after you were born, I gained weight. I was exhausted from carrying you and giving you birth."

"Why didn't you and daddy ever have more children?"

More tears fell. Beth suspected her mother might have miscarried and it drained her. "I miscarried. Two years after you were born I lost my baby. Your dad thought it best not to try again."

Both finished drying off and putting their clothes on, but this piece of news left a big hole in her heart. "I would have had a baby sister or brother?"

Ann gave a faint smile. "Brother, yes."

Beth felt a wave of sympathy coming over her. She would have had a younger brother. Dad would have loved having a son. In her years of growing up, she'd never seen her father depressed. She admired his strength. Perhaps her mother was what he needed. She completed him. She had few memories of her dad spending time with her, but she knew he loved her. "Oh, mother. Was dad sad?"

"You know how men are. They keep their feelings to themselves."

Speaking of men, Stan left with Larry. Her heart dropped into her chest. She hoped she could have said hi or apologize for being aloof, but maybe another day. Now, she wanted to stay with her mother. Beth appreciated her mother after learning her mother miscarried. "You're ready to go home, mom?"

Her mother nodded.

Beth followed her mother to the lockers and they took out their personal belongings and headed for the register. She surprised her mother when she said, "I'd like to come back in the morning as you suggested."

She raised her eyebrows, giving Beth a questionable gaze. "You mean it?

She nodded. "Workout was good today."

Her hopefulness turned to disbelief. "Did I hear right?"

"You did. It invigorated me. Hard work but invigorating."

"Last week, you didn't want to. I'm glad I insisted." She smiled.

As they headed out to Ann's car, Stan stood by his car and talked to his friend. What were they discussing? Men were not as emotional as women were. On her last date, he spoke of his job and how good Beth looked in her yellow dress. He said nothing else.

"You're staring at him."

"I thought we could talk." Beth watched him get into his car. He only said hello or gave her a smile when they walked in. Her stomach clenched.

"It would be too late to ask you out for coffee."

"I know." She shook off her disappointment. If Stan was for her, he would have tried.

"And you gave him an impression you weren't interested in him."

Guilt hung over her head like a dark cloud. Her mother was right. She could move on, at least. "Lord, if he is for me, give me a sign." She prayed.

*****

Stan waited for Beth to walk out of the gym, but Larry suggested they should head home.

"I was going to ask if she would come to church with me tomorrow."

"She probably attends elsewhere. Besides, she may reject you."

Stan frowned. “I thought for sure something had changed. The way she looked at me told me she had second thoughts.”

“The Good Lord will give you another chance with her.”

“I hope so.” He climbed into his car and drove home, following Larry in his car.

Stan turned the radio on to soft music. Besides Christian music, he loved listening to piano music. He took some deep breaths and relaxed. “Lord, I had a good workout. Good to see Beth there too.” The few times he glimpsed her way, her demeanor was different. Something about her appealed to him. What was it? He would love to find out.

Beth never gave him her phone number. He could stop by the other bookstore and ask to have lunch with her. Yes, he wanted to know her more.

Ten

Beth walked into the bookstore and headed for the back room. While Jenna usually worked the register, her employer had stationed herself there.

"Where's Jodi?"

"She's not coming in. Can you handle the register until Jenna arrives?"

"Yes. Let me clock in first."

"Okay."

She could work the register. While she was still new at the bookstore, she had similar experiences at her last two jobs. She signed her name in and the time she reported coming in and ambled to the register. She took a slow and easy breath as she stepped behind the register.

A woman and her young daughter walked in and browsed the aisles of books. She stepped out from her register and approached the two. "Can I help you?"

The woman looked up and smiled. "Oh, we are just browsing. Thanks."

"No problem. If you need anything, let me know. How old is your daughter?"

"Eight."

"I'll be behind the register." She walked to her station as a customer approached her. Beth scanned the bar code on the two books, bookmarks and the audiobook and totaled the prices.

"Do you know when Stephen Fisher's new book would be out?"

"Let me check." She put his items in a bag. "First, your total is fifty-nine dollars and eighty-five cents." She stared at the man and froze. The man had the same colored eyes as Drew.

He's not Drew.

Beth relaxed and gave him a coy smile. She returned to his question and checked the dates for new arrivals. "Yes, the book will be out next Thursday."

"Okay, I'll be here."

"Are you a fast reader? Those books are not short." She pointed to his purchases.

"One is a gift. My best friend has a birthday coming up and the other is mine." He smiled.

Her heart fluttered. He had an amazing smile, but her lack of confidence in herself caused her heart to sink. He wouldn't be interested in her. "You have a favorite author? Let me guess. Stephen Fisher?"

"Yes. Have you read anything by him?"

She frowned. "I'm not into psychological thrillers."

He gave her his credit card. "Touché. I've read all of his books."

She put his card through the machine. "Maybe your girlfriend likes him."

"Don't have one."

Her eyes widened. "That's a shame. Maybe you'll find one who likes Stephen Fisher."

"I think I have found one already. Would you go out with me?"

His question stopped her in her tracks. “But I don’t like psychological thrillers.” She giggled.

“I like you.”

Nothing was set in stone with her friendship with Stan. Although they were both Christians and work in bookstores, she immediately felt more comfortable with this guy.

You were comfortable with Brad.

Brad was different. Brad didn’t care that she was fat. She still needed to work on her weight, but her demeanor this morning had changed. Could she trust him? Would he turn out to be another Brad?

“What do you say?”

She studied him. The customer had blue eyes, but they weren’t steely blue. He didn’t have dark hair either. Drew wouldn’t know where to locate her. Why not give this guy a chance? “What’s your name?”

“John Parker.”

Her heart raced. Wasn’t there an author named John Parker? She needed to study author pics on the back of the books.

“And you are,” he said, reading her name tag, “Beth Miller. Nice to meet you, Beth.”

“I think there is a customer waiting behind you.” Beth smiled to the customer.

He took out a pen and scribbled his number on a piece of paper. “Call me if you would like lunch with me. I will be working on a novel at home.” He handed the paper to her then left.

She watched him leave. Was he playing with her? His interest in her had to be a joke. Her breath caught in her chest. She didn't know what to make of the invitation. On the outside, he was a nice man but, on the inside, —what if he was laughing at her?

He thinks you're desperate.

"I would have to pray." She felt trapped. She wanted to believe the best, but fear kept her from believing his sincerity. What a stark contrast between him and Stan!

"Do you even know who he is?" Her co-worker took her out of her thoughts.

"Yes, he told me. I'm just wondering why he would ask me out."

"Yeah, me too. You're lucky!" Angelique walked away, laughing.

Trying not show her hurt, she lifted her chin as she continued at the register.

When Jodi arrived, she relieved her, but stopped her when she noticed Beth's demeanor. "What happened?" Jodi wasn't mean like Angelique. Jodi took her on as a friend and co-worker. Was Jodi a Christian? She doubted Angelique was, by her attitude.

Beth glanced around, seeing Angelique nearby. "I think Angelique has contempt for me. She didn't like John Parker asking me out on a date."

Jodi's hands flew to her chest as her eyes widened. "He was here? He asked you out?"

"Yes. Can you believe he would ask me? You two ladies are more attractive than me–"

"Don't say that! We are all attractive in our own ways. I've seen people a lot worse than you."

Her cheeks felt warm. "Aww. Thank you."

"And you may be right. John has been here once but for book signings. Did he come in here looking for a date?" She looked her square in the eye as she placed her hands on her hips.

"He brought some items. Asked me about a certain book."

"Did you say yes?" She glanced past Beth and then at her. "Hello, Angel."

"She let you call her Angel?"

"Yes."

"Hmm. I better get to my assigned place."

"All right."

******

One more hour and he could break for lunch. Stan saw Beth briefly at the gym, but she finished while he turned on the shower. He gave her a quick smile, then, before she headed out.

His heart warmed. He couldn't wait to see her. What time did she break for lunch? Maybe he could have lunch with her.

"Wow, Stan! Did something happen to you?" his supervisor asked.

"Not exactly. Just thinking how Beth looked today. May I take an early lunch break?"

"No. Hannah has one at 11, then you break."

Being a male among female employees didn't bother Stan, and Hannah was nice. Down to earth, but she had a man in her life. Stan didn't find satisfaction in a bookstore.

He liked books, but how long would he have to shelve books and price them? Should he find a job elsewhere?

He went back to his station.

You could try mission work.

Mission work? A month ago, a missionary from Greece spoke at his church. He felt the tug in his heart but pushed the tug aside. Fear got in the way. He wanted to stay in California. He wasn't called to do mission work. His parents weren't missionaries. He didn't feel qualified.

I qualify you.

What about Beth? He would not have a chance to build a relationship with her. Worse yet, she could forget him and date someone else. Wait? Dating? Why was he thinking that when they were only friends?

"I'll contact my pastor later."

"Beg your pardon?" A customer quizzed him as she passed by. She stopped in her tracks. "Oh, hi, Stan! Why did you want to call our pastor?" Anita. Of course, he would recognize the church secretary. "Hi, Anita. You remember the missionary from Greece? He said he needed more people to help out."

"I remember. My nineteen-year-old daughter is going there." A smile spread across her face. "If the Lord is calling you, you should heed. Call the pastor as soon as you can."

"Thanks, I will." Did the Lord send Anita as an answer to prayer? Anita had never come into the store prior to that day. Anita had such a heart for the Lord. She faithfully served as the church secretary for ten years. He admired the older woman.

When it was time for his lunch break, he took out his phone and called Larry to meet him at Wendy's. "I need to discuss something with you."

"Wow! Sounds important."

"My news is important, and it could affect my friendship with Beth." He wanted to set Larry up with Beth, but the Lord convinced him. He would have to trust God.

"I can be there in ten minutes."

"Great! Meet you there." He ended the call.

The town had one Wendy's and it would not take them long to arrive. He headed for his Prius and began his short drive

Eleven

The line at Wendy's was a little too long for his taste. He checked his watch. He had an hour- long lunch break; otherwise, he'd have gone elsewhere. A two-year-old boy stared at him as his mother held him in his arms. He gave the little tyke a smile and a wave. "Hi!"

The woman smiled and giggled. "Don't mind him. He loves to stare."

"How old is he?"

"Two and a half."

"Is he your only one?"

"I have a six-year-old in school."

"Ahh."

"Hey!" A tap on his shoulder and he jerked, but he smiled at his friend. "Sorry."

"It's okay."

"So, what happened? Beth visited your workplace?"

"Not yet, but I may stop by after lunch break and say hi."

Larry took his place behind Stan as the line moved. "Long line."

He checked his watch. "I know."

Beth and a blonde-headed woman waited in the next line. "I know the Lord wants us together. When she is in the same place as me, I don't think it's coincidence."

Larry glanced at the women, then him. “Who’s the other blonde?”

“I have no idea.”

Beth stared at him, then whispered to her friend. Her friend smiled.

*****

“Don’t tell me he likes Wendy’s too!” Holly said to Beth. “He’s cute.”

“Cute? Not sure men like being called cute.”

“Good looking.”

“I like him—Oh, did I tell you John Parker asked me out?”

“The author? That’s great!” Holly stared at Larry.

“You like Larry?”

“The man next to Stan is Larry?” “

“Yes. What happened to Clint?”

“He’s seeing someone else.”

“I’m sorry to hear that.”

“Does Larry live in the country?”

“No. He shares an apartment with Stan.”

“Welcome to Wendy’s. What I can get you?”

****

Larry stared off into space. Or was he gawking? Beth’s friend was pretty, and Larry could ask her out if he wasn’t a confirmed bachelor. Should he invite them over to his table?

Beth walked toward the dining area and sat in a chair. He was glad Beth decided to eat here too. He needed to talk to her and Larry showed interest in her friend. This could work out. He smiled until Beth stared his way. "You're up next," the employee called out.

His face felt hot as he turned and cleared his throat. "I will have the apple pecan salad with a large Coke." Normally he wouldn't have a soda. The aspartame wasn't good for the body, but he was at Wendy's and not A Fresh Start.

"Will that be all?" the friendly female clerk asked..

"Yes. Thank you."

She totaled the price on her register. "$7.35."

He gave her a ten and she gave him his receipt. "I'm going to introduce myself to her friend."

"Okay."

Stan headed for Beth's table and waved to her. "I'm glad you are here."

"Holly, this is Stan; I met him at the gym."

"But you're not dating?" she asked, looking at him.

"We're just friends," Stan replied. "Nice to meet you."

"Likewise."

"I haven't seen you before?"

"I'm visiting Beth; I live on a farm not far from here."

"So, your parents are farmers?"

"My dad is. My mother died when I was twelve."

"I'm sorry to hear that."

Holly stared past Stan. "Hi. You are?"

"Larry. Larry Anderson. Nice to meet you."

"Holly Hawthorne"

He offered her a warm smile. "You want to join us?"

"Beth?"

"I…guess."

"Order number 15."

"That's me." Beth then left the table.

Holly followed the two men to another table. "So, Larry. What do you do?"

"I sell car parts."

"Like at NAPA?"

"Yes. And you? I could tell you are not a city girl."

"I help my father on the farm."

"Are you seeing anyone, Holly?"

Stan's mouth flew open in surprise. Did he really hear what he thought he just heard?

"Not at the moment." She smiled

"She just got out of a relationship." Beth sat down with her order.

"Oh?"

"Yes, but we are still friends." She stared at Beth. "Like you and Beth."

"So, what did you want to tell me?" Beth took a sandwich out of her bag and Stan held back his disappointment.

"I would like to know—how would me leaving for Greece affect our friendship."

"Why are you going there?" She put a straw in her drink.

"First, I felt I could do more in my job. I have been shelving books and pricing them and sometimes reviewing books for over five years. The Lord reminded me of a call for mission work in Greece."

"That's great! You should go."

His stomach clenched. Her response surprised him, but it shouldn't have. His eyes drifted toward Larry. Thoughts of his roommate with Beth filled his mind. Yet he shook those thoughts aside. Larry was interested in Holly, not Beth. Lord, help me to respond to her reaction. "You want me to respond to the call? We won't have a chance to build up our friendship."

"I'll still be here when you return."

"I could be in Greece a long time."

"But if the Lord wants you to go, you should. You wouldn't want to displease Him."

She was pushing him away. He pressed his lips but swallowed his pride; he then forced a smile on his face. Although he loved her love for the Lord, he couldn't help but think she was using the Lord to say "I'm not interested in you."

"Okay, but not because you said so."

She smiled.

After all, they were friends.

Larry and Holly were talking to each other. The first time Larry was at ease with a woman. Holly said she came out of a relationship. What caused the relationship to end? "Larry came out of a failed marriage," he told Beth.

"What happened?"

"Not my place to tell you, but I hope Larry and Holly will date each other."

"I hope Larry likes farm girls. From what Holly tells me, Clint left the farming community for a job in the city."

"Sounds like Larry. Larry lived on the farm until he was eighteen."

Her mouth dropped open and her eyes grew big. "He doesn't strike me as a country boy."

"He's lived in the city for 14 years."

"Why?" She took a bite of her sandwich.

"Order number 20!"

"That's me." He got up from his seat.

"How long have you been farming?" Larry asked.

"Since I was born. My father was a third-generation farmer." She yawned. "What's it like living in the city? You ever get tired of the city?" Holly asked.

"I have friends who live on the ranch," Beth interjected. "She was a city girl married to a country boy. You might be next." Thoughts of her friend sprung hope in her heart.

"I grew up on the farm," Larry replied.

"Yes, he did." Stan sat with his order.

"You told me. Of course."

"Wow! What brought you to the city?" Holly asked.

"I wanted more than what the farm had to offer." And he told Holly the same thing Stan told Beth.

"If you are interested in dating a country girl, give me a call." She wrote her number on a piece of paper.

"Have you changed your mind, my friend?" Stan asked.

"She's nice, but I need to pray."

"You can start as friends."

"Of course."

Twelve

Stan spoke to his pastor on the phone about working in Greece as a missionary.

"I'm glad you finally listened to the Lord," his pastor said.

Stan's heart raced. "What are you saying?"

"I saw your face the day the missionary spoke, but it took you this long to accept the call."

If he had answered the call sooner, he would not have met Beth. Now he could relax, knowing that Beth was in God's hand and Larry was interested in Holly.

But why was he worried? When he told her, she perplexed him. She wanted him to go! Did she not want to build a relationship? How could they do that if he is a missionary in Greece?

"What's on your mind, son?" His pastor broke through his thoughts.

"There is this woman I am interested in. I told her about the call and she said I should accept the call. I thought she would miss me."

"Maybe she isn't spending her life thinking about you. Is she a Christian?"

"Yes."

"Give her to God. The scripture says to seek God and his ways, and he will add unto you all those things you long to pursue."

"Including a woman?"

"Yes. Let God take care of the rest."

"Okay."

"Visit my office and we will get the paperwork going."

"I work the next day. Can I visit after work?"

"I'll see you Sunday Morning."

"Okay." He ended the call.

Where would he get the money? He went to his room to pray. His roommate was in the next room strumming a guitar, but the music wasn't going to distract him. In fact, the music helped him to focus.

Kneeling at his bed, he closed his eyes. "Lord, help me raise the money to do your work in Greece. Prepare me for what's ahead."

Waiting in the silence, a song poured through the walls, coming from the outer room. Larry was singing a hymn. "Have thine own way, Lord. Have thy own will…"

He used to sing it years ago in church, but Larry had never played hymns on his guitar. His breath hitched. Where was the music coming from? He got up from the floor and quietly walked to the door.

"…While I am waiting yielded and still…"

Not to make a sound, he crept his way to the next room.

"Have thy own way, Lord. Have thy own way…"

Stan pushed the door a little.

"Come in, Stan!" Larry called out.

Stan grinned. "What were you playing?"

"A classic. Somehow, I felt led to play this song." He stared at his guitar, then at Stan. "But I have never learned to play it."

Stan crossed his arms. And wiggled his eyebrows. "Really?"

"The truth. Why?"

"I was praying, and the song poured through my walls."

"Sorry to bother you."

"I'll go back to praying." He clamped his lips together to keep from laughing. Stan was no musician, but he knew…unless the Holy Spirit was involved. He lifted his eyes. "God?"

Back in his room, he returned to waiting on the Lord.

*****

The ladies arrived at Beth's house. Her mother's car was absent from the driveway and Beth relaxed. After an unnerving lunch at Wendy's she could now enjoy her time with Holly. She had forgotten about Holly until her friend called.

"Okay, God. You are trying to say something." She turned off her engine. "What? He's going to Greece, isn't he?"

She felt mildly disappointed when he shared his news, but his new plan released her from seeing him again. Where would he get the money? God, of course; and if God wanted him to go to Greece, He would provide. No need to worry. She wanted him to accept the call.

Use whatever time you have, to cultivate your friendship with him.

"But if I do, we will miss each other later."

You wanted to see less of him, didn't you?

She shifted in her seat and grimaced. Yes, He was right. Beth stared out the window. "Because…I'm not attracted to him." She confessed.

What else?

"I'm afraid our friendship will lead to dating."

Don't blame your mother or Larry.

"You put it in my mom's and Larry's heart?"

A knock on the door interrupted her prayer. She directed her attention to Holly standing outside, looking in. "Are you ready?"

"Of course." She smiled to her friend. She would get her answer later, although He had told her.

Beth opened her door and climbed out. "I was talking to the Lord concerning Stan."

"He seems nice."

"So, you're interested in Larry?" She walked to her house.

"I like him." Holly sounded hopeful.

"Enough to date him?"

"He hasn't asked me out."

Beth smirked. Holly was thin and as attractive as Larry. They could be perfect, but Larry lived in the city. Beth could adjust to living in the country.

You were once interested in a married cowboy and now you want to take Larry away from Holly.

Beth frowned. Did her conscience have to bother her? Did He have to remind her?

"What's wrong, Beth? Don't you like Larry?"

Beth removed her key from her purse. Every time she liked someone, he was either using her or he was married. Why did God choose Stan for her? "Yes, I like him a lot, but Stan told me he is not open to dating. I want to spare you."

"That's fine. Not sure he would want to live on a farm." Her voice hinted disappointment. Beth lowered her eyes.

After unlocking the door, she led her friend in. "What time do you have to be home? Don't you have to feed the animals?"

"Did that this morning." She followed her to the living room and glanced around. "Nice house. Did you get a place of your own?"

"I did once. Long story if you want to hear it."

A country tune chimed, and Holly took her cell phone out of her pocket and she answered. "Hello ... Hi, dad. I'm at Beth's house… It would take hour to get home. Can you wait an hour...? I'll be there." She ended the call. "I guess I can't stay, but I'll visit you Saturday and we can chat."

"I would like that. Thanks for stopping by."

Holly reached in to give Beth a hug as Beth's mother pulled into the driveway. "Your mother is home."

Beth smiled. "She normally comes home now. See you later, Holly."

Holly walked to her car and waved to Ann. "Bye, Ms. Miller!"

Beth climbed out and met her mother at the door. "You won't ever guess what happened today." She followed her mother in.

"You saw Stan."

Beth rolled her eyes. Of course, her mother would say that. "John Parker asked me out on a date."

"Who?" She looked puzzled as she led Beth to the kitchen. "What would you like for dinner? Whole wheat tacos or whole wheat spaghetti made with fresh ingredients?"

Beth grimaced. "Whole wheat?"

"Yep. No bleached flour for us."

"Shouldn't I eat what I want?" She crossed her arms.

"Sure, but I thought we both were on a diet, right?"

"We are, but I can make choices."

"Buy your own food." She opened the refrigerator. "So, who is John Parker?"

"An author. He writes psychological thrillers."

"Is he a Christian? I like Stan." She pulled out a bag of grated cheese, light sour cream, tomatoes and lettuce.

Of course, she does. "I don't know. I didn't accept either. Jodi thinks I should, but Angelica wished he had asked her." She sat at the bar. "So, have you been seeing anyone? Like from church?"

"Too busy working to date." She reached for the box of tacos shells from the cabinet.

"I work too but I could find time to date."

Her mother glanced at Beth "You have a date with Stan?" Hope was in her eyes.

"He is going to Greece as a missionary."

"Greece? When is that?"

"I don't know."

"Well, depending on his church, Stan has time before he leaves for Greece. Why not take the opportunity to get to know him before he leaves? Who knows, you could work with him. Wouldn't that be exciting?" She stepped off the stool and took out a skillet.

"Building a relationship takes time...that's if I am interested." She sighed. God told her it was His idea. Suddenly, she felt empty. Had she truly surrendered her will to the Lord?

"Have thy own way, Lord…" her mother sung.

Beth shot her mother a look as her mouth opened. "I was thinking that!" And yet she didn't voice her thought.

Her mother gave her a big smile. "Just a song that came to my mind."

"I haven't heard that song in years; since we left Grace Baptist Church."

"I miss Grace Baptist."

What church did Stanley attend? She would have to ask. First a phone call. She took a phone out and dialed his number.

"Who are you calling, sweetheart?"

Beth smiled. Her answer would please her mom. "Stanley."

Her mother squealed with abject delight.

******

The phone had rung, and his heart raced. Thinking his pastor was calling him, he ran to the phone and answered. "Hello?"

"Hi. This is Beth. Hey, I was just wondering something. What church do you attend?"

Hearing her voice warmed his heart and his skin tingled, yet he remained calm. "Hi, Beth. I attend North Valley Fellowship Center. Are you interested in attending?"

"With my new friend," she replied in her sweet voice.

His heart soared. "I would love that! I attend Bible study at 8:30, but the service starts at 10. You know where we meet?"

"I've seen the building. Bible study starts at 8:30?"

"8:45."

"Aww. Can I meet you there?"

"Beth, I'd be more than glad to take you with me."

"Since we are not dating, let's just meet. Okay?"

She didn't want to go anywhere with him. Beth didn't sound like she was interested in dating, but he offered friendship, not a relationship. Why didn't she want him to take her? He imagined the congregation asking if she was his girlfriend. He would have to tell the truth. "Any reason you don't want me to take you there?" He pressed his lips, hoping for a favorable answer.

"Don't you think it's reasonable?"

"For a friend to drive a friend?"

"A female friend?"

Beth was curious. She wanted to check out the place where he worshiped. His fellow members might not question him if they arrived separately. "You're right. I hope to see you there. Are you going to the gym tomorrow by any chance?"

She sighed. "Yes. Mom is coming with me. I agreed to work out every day with her now."

"What time do you arrive in the morning?" A man and woman walked by the house, holding hands.

"Six. We were late this morning."

"Ah. That was why I didn't see you come in when I did."

"When did you arrive today?"

"Seven."

She giggled. "I guess you'll be there tomorrow."

"Bright and early." He chuckled.

"Bye."

"Bye." He hit end call. He stared up into heaven and said, "Thank you, God!"

Thirteen

At the corner of 10th street and Park place, cars filled the parking lot, but she found one between a white Ford truck and a white Prius. Didn't Stan drive a Prius? "We'll find out." She squeezed out of her car into the tight space and followed the people walking toward the building. She didn't know which class he was in until he stood in front of a classroom. He waited for me!

"I figured you wouldn't know which room. We have Sunday school for kids to high-school age, a young adult class and two adult classes. You're welcome to attend mine with me"

"I might as well." She followed him inside.

Inside, chairs lined up in a row. At her Sunday school, they sat at tables, but not this one. Members sat toward the back and the front, leaving the second, third and fourth rows to choose from. She sighed and chose a chair in the third row.

A man leaned over to her. "Hi. Remember me?"

Her heart raced. The voice sounded familiar. John? She glanced back. "So, you are?"

"I am what?" He smiled.

"I never thought to ask if you are a Christian."

"A new one. I recently accepted Christ five months ago."

"Sorry I didn't call you, but I found it hard to believe you would be interested in me."

*****

The conversation between John Parker and Beth intrigued Stan. How did she know him? He grabbed a seat on the other side of John and watched them talk.

"I am." He glanced at Stan. "You know him? I saw you coming in with him."

"Stan and I are friends. I've been saved since I was a little girl, but I had walked away from my faith when a former boyfriend persuaded me to join his cult."

His mouth dropped open. "You joined a cult?"

"Yes, but not for long. After he abused me, I left him. God gave me the strength to leave him and his cult."

"Wow! I heard they are hard to get out."

"I had praying friends and a praying mother."

He smiled.

Stan folded his arms. She had shared more with John than him. Had he gone at it the wrong way? He attempted a smile to hide his bitterness. "Beth and I met recently. We both work at a bookstore."

"You work at her competition?"

"Not my choosing, but yes." Should he tell him where he met her? Would telling him attract John to her, knowing she is working on losing weight?

"Good morning, class." The instructor refocused everyone's attention to the front. "We'll start with announcements. Tonight, at six, we have an evening service. Pastor Jason will be preaching from the book of Revelations. In the bulletin, there is an insert announcing a baby shower for Jenna Conrad." She pointed to a woman seated near the front, sitting next to her husband'. "And don't forget Wednesday night's Bible studies, which is in the bulletin."

She glanced around and at Beth. "We have a guest! Welcome. We are glad you could join us."

"Thanks." Beth said.

"Why don't we pray before we begin?"

After Bible study, Beth tried to leave quietly. The welcome made her face flush and she wanted to hide. Now she hoped no one would stop her.... except maybe John or Stan.

John. Her life just got more interesting. While he was new to the faith, she liked him. Her heart told her not to judge on appearance and reminded her of giving Stan a chance at friendship. Yet her eyes lit up when he said hello to her. "Couldn't I be friends with both men?"

Stan caught up with her. "So, you like John?"

"I like you too." She wanted to soften the blow. "I like both of you."

"I'm not jealous.... well, maybe a little. How did you get lucky to meet someone like him?"

"I don't know. I'm really not interested in him." She gazed at him. "You want to sit together in service?"

He reached out but retracted his hand. "Yes."

Beth followed him to the sanctuary.

As they made their way into the lobby, Stan introduced her as his friend. Their eyes lit up and their mouths curved upward. Did they know something?

"Glad you found a woman for yourself, Stan," an usher said.

"We're just friends, Norman," he said as he shook his hand. "Beth, this is Norman. He's one of the ushers."

"Hi," she said.

Once inside the sanctuary, Beth relaxed, and he smiled. "I'm sorry they asked. I haven't had a woman in my life so it's a big deal to them."

"How long have you attended service here?"

"Since my conversion. Larry brought me here."

She scanned the room. "Where is he?"

"He should be here." He spotted Larry toward the front, but instead of taking her there, he let her choose. "Where would you like to sit?"

"You can sit with your friend. You don't have to be with me."

"But I want to. I would much rather be with you than him."

Her face glowed. "Over here." She pointed toward a row in the back and he figured she would "Holly told me she likes him."

"He likes her too."

She gasped. "I thought he wasn't into dating."

"He isn't. They may be friends for now."

"Oh, okay."

He let her scoot in first, then he kept space between them. He realized she wasn't here for him, but to check out his church. He prayed she would want to attend again. "Where do you and your mother attend church?"

"First Assembly of God."

His heart fluttered. Although his church was nondenominational, her faith was similar to his. God had given another sign. "That's great!"

****

Beth glanced around, trying to keep the butterflies under control. She checked the time on her watch. The service would start in ten minutes. The people walking by their pew didn't seem to notice her next to him. A couple glanced past her over to Stan.

"Hey, Stan! How are you?" A man asked.

"Great! Have you met my friend Beth?" He stared up at him.

Great. Bring her to his attention. She wanted to hide. Next to Stan, she felt like a fat pig. When his friend glanced at her, he said, "Hello, Beth. Nice to meet you."

Over in the distance, John scooted into a back row on the other side. She caught herself smiling to him and glanced away. Don't give him the impression you're interested.

Beth busied herself by looking at the worship guide the greeter gave her. Lots of activities going on this week. Evening service under the stars? Were they having an old-fashioned revival? Fit for Life Bible study. Did Stan attend Fit for Life? She glanced at him. *Ask him.*

No. She wasn't going to ask. Why should she? She's not a member of this congregation.

The music started, and she jumped.

Stan chuckled. "Nervous?"

"Me? Nervous? A fat girl attending church with you and I'm nervous?" She gave a nervous laugh.

"You wanted to come."

Funny. An accusing thought had told her she wanted to come. She shook off the thought. "I know. I didn't expect us in the same pew together."

John glanced her way. Great. Now he thinks I'm seeing Stan.

You are. A voice told her.

Shut up!

"Good morning! God is good!" The man in front said.

"All the time." The congregation responded.

"If this is your first, second, or third time, I invite you to fill out the connection card that is in front of you."

Beth reached to the rack and took out the card. She filled these out before when she visited Julie in Montana. She wished she wasn't so gullible. Her desperation had caused her to make a foolish decision. Loretta and Roy gave her a chance, but she blew her chance.

The worship team played a song and everyone around her stood. Stan offered his hand and she accepted. What was she doing with a man? Her eyes darted everywhere. Were people looking at her? Laughing? She tried not to let the stares bother her. She gave it to Jesus.

******

"Are you okay, Beth?" Stan asked.

"She may have been nervous," Larry said.

She gave a sweet smile to the men. "I'm fine." She continued to lift her hands up in worship.

"Maybe she felt singled out. Ask her after church."

When the time of worship ended, the members sat in their seats, and Beth relaxed. Stan didn't know why she was nervous. The people here were friendly. He stared at his friend and not seeing Holly next to him, he asked him a pointed question. "You didn't invite Holly to Church?"

"She went back to her father's farm. They attend a Baptist church."

"Southern Baptist, no doubt," Stan said.

"The attendance there is about 60, but Holly is comfortable with small membership," Beth explained to Sam. "Farmers and ranchers attend the church."

"How did you meet Holly?"

"If I haven't told you, I'll tell you later." She stared toward the front.

The deacons came to their row and Beth took the collection plate and put in a five. She smiled as she passed the plate to him.

She's a giver! Another sign from the Lord. However, he didn't get any vibe from her that she was ready to date.

Later the pastor preached his sermon on the feeding of five thousand…

Fourteen

As soon as the service ended, Beth dashed out of the sanctuary as if a swarm of bees were chasing her. Stan scratched his head. Didn't she enjoy the service? "She acted funny."

"It wasn't you," Larry assured him. "Did you bring her here?"

"No. She wanted to check out the church."

"That's a good sign! She is interested in you."

Stanley shook his head as he doubted it. She had put distance between then, sitting close to the end of the pew.

"Where did she attend service?"

"First Assembly of God."

"Awesome! You'll see her again."

His heart warmed. "I know." He followed his friend out to the parking lot. "Meet you at the apartment."

"I'm driving to the country to see Holly."

"For reals?" He jerked.

"For reals. I'm glad I met her. Thank Beth for me." He climbed into his car.

A blue Toyota parked next to his Prius. "Beth?" He peered in and smiled at her. Beth hadn't left. He knocked on the window.

Beth jumped, nearly bumping her head on the ceiling of the car. She glared at him as he tried to tried to hold back a chuckle. She rolled down her window. "What do you want?"

"Did you know you parked next to my car?" He grinned.

"So? Only spot I could find," she retorted.

"Or God directed you to this spot."

"Maybe." She sighed.

"As friends, would you have lunch with me?"

"I…I don't know. My mom may expect me home for lunch."

"I think she wouldn't mind."

She stared out her front window and grimaced.

"I don't bite."

"I'm sorry. Maybe another day." She glanced at him.

"See you at the gym tomorrow."

"Okay."

Beth watched him climbed into his car, waiting for him to leave. She hoped he wouldn't find her. How she to know the white Prius was was his? She stared up into heaven. "Was he right, God? Did you have me park here? Should I take him up on his offer?"

She intended to check out his church and sit alone. She shook her head. *I shouldn't have come.* And John attended his church too? She covered her head with her hands.

Her cell phone chimed in her purse. She retrieved her phone and her mother's caller ID displayed on her screen. "Mom?"

"How was service where you attended this morning?"

"Ummm.... good." Should she tell her she saw John? Her mom was all for Stanley.

"Do you think you'll attend again?"

"I don't know. Are you expecting me home for lunch?"

"Actually, that's why I called. I'm having company over."

Beth couldn't breathe. "You are? "Who?"

"The Reverend and his wife. I invited them over."

"Why? I mean they visit new members."

"I asked them over. Will you be coming?"

Suddenly having lunch with Stan appealed to her. If she told her mom, would she tell her to accept the invitation? "Actually, I have other plans. Stan asked me to have lunch with him."

"Oh, Beth! That's great! Go have lunch with Stan."

She knew it. Now she would have to call him and tell him she changed her mind.

A red sports car drove past her view. She hardly made out the driver, but she suspected the driver was John. Despite turning him down, he talked to her. She could be wrong. He did give her his number. Angelique. Better not. Although John was a new Christian, he could treat her as nothing. I'll call Stan, she thought. "Okay, I will." She ended the call and hit redial on her phone.

"Hello."

"I changed my mind and you were right. In fact, she is expecting company."

"What was I right about, Beth?"

"She told me to have lunch with you."

"Would you like to eat at A Fresh Start?"

"I guess." They both—well, her mom and her liked eating there. Since they are both dieting, her mother chose healthy alternatives such as A Fresh Start.

He chuckled. "You guess. You have anywhere else in mind?"

Across the street from the parking lot was a seafood restaurant. She wouldn't have to drive. She could wait for him. How far was he from the church? "Do you eat seafood?"

"Yes."

"How about the one across from your church?"

"You are still at the church, aren't you?"

"Yes."

"I'll be there in ten minutes."

"Take your time." She hit end call and took a deep breath. "I can't believe I am doing this! Am I going to see more of him?"

Yes.

"Thanks for the response, God." She said with feigned enthusiasm.

******

After getting off the phone, he stared up to heaven. "Lord, you are good! Our friendship will continue to grow."

But his excitement faded when he remembered his meeting with the pastor. He met with him before Beth arrived at church. He had told his pastor that Beth would attend a service here.

"It's serious now?"

"We're still friends. She is checking out the church."

"We'll welcome her. As for going to Greece, will you still work as a missionary?

"Yes."

"Okay. I have called Brian and Rhianna Harris and they are going to connect with you. You will need to complete training, learn the language et cetera. This takes time and may not be immediate."

"Okay."

"Who knows, maybe by the time you start, you and Beth will be married, and she could accompany you."

"One day at a time. She is uncomfortable around me."

"If she is the one, God will prepare both of you."

"Okay."

Stan had told Beth he planned to become a missionary for Greece. She was excited, of course, but would her excitement change if they got more involved with each other? God knows.

He had driven past two blocks when she called. He made a U turn and drove back toward the church. "God, you are working this out, but I think she is fighting. And there is that author fellow. I don't think I have a chance if he is in the picture." He's glad they won't send him to Greece all that soon His pastor was right. They could work together. "Prepare her, Lord."

Her blue Toyota wasn't anywhere in sight until she walked across the street on a green light. She hadn't left the church. Was she praying? His heart warmed.

She is still insecure regarding her weight.

Stan was at two hundred pounds years ago. Obesity causes people to have low self-esteem. "Help her to see I accept her." Stan wasn't vain either. He wanted to treat her the way he wasn't treated years ago, even now.

As she neared the restaurant, his heart palpitated. He climbed out of his car. "Beth."

She glanced his way. "Hi. My mother invited our pastor and his wife. I chose you." She smiled.

"I love your dress. It looks nice on you."

Her face reddened. "Thank you. That's nice of you to say so."

Well done, Stanley.

"You're welcome. Shall we?" He led her inside.

"Did you tell your pastor you wanted to work as a missionary?" She followed him to the waiting area.

"Yes, I met with him before you arrived this morning. He told me the process would take months and I would have to learn the language."

"You can learn the language"

"Curious. Have you wanted to travel to another country?"

"When I was a little girl, I wanted to visit my pen pal in Greece."

His heart raced. Was this another sign? The sign from God? "Have you been in touch with her?"

"I lost touch 12 years ago. They moved to the Ukraine, which was the last I heard of her. Why?"

"Welcome to Sea Food World," a hostess said, coming toward them. "How many in your party?"

"Two," Stanley said.

The hostess took out two menus. "Smoking or non-smoking?"

Does Beth smoke? He used to smoke long ago, but he didn't know if Beth smokes.

"I don't smoke."

Thank you, God.

******

What could they talk about? The service? Her insecurities? They discussed Greece. Her breath hitched. What else did they discuss in the meeting? When the hostess returned, she asked him, "what happened in the meeting?"

"He is going to connect me with Brian and Rhianna from church."

She opened the menu. "Since we are friends–"

"Let me pay for your meal since I'm the one who asked you out."

Her pulse raced. "Were you going to say date?"

"Beth, about John…are you interested in him? I'm curious."

"Look at me, Stanley! Am I dating material for a famous author? And because he happened to attend your church, that doesn't mean he is a true Christian."

"He did accept Christ five months ago."

"Well, if I am interested in anyone, I wouldn't be here, would I?"

"What are you saying?"

"I'm not a two timer. John asked me out, but I never accepted. You asked me out…"

"And you accepted."

"Reluctantly. I accepted because…. I like you."

He wanted to drink in this moment. He wasn't sure how or what she thought of him. The first time, she ran out on him. A transformation must have happened. She blossomed. "I know if I had lunch with my mother, they would be talking back and forth. My mother likes to talk—what?"

"Seems as you got that from your mother. No offense."

"None taken." She took a drink of her water. "I guess I'm feeling comfortable around you."

"And this morning?"

"Nerves. I'm not comfortable with my weight. I weighed myself. Lost one pound."

"That's great!"

"I wish I had lost more."

"No, don't wish that. I learned the hard way I would end up gaining it back. Keep on working out and eating right."

"My mother would agree. She lost two pounds." She gave him a blank look.

"When I started my journey, I didn't lose weight right away and it was hard. I gave up smoking, which was why I gained weight."

"Smoking suppressed your appetite?"

"Yes. I had other problems too, Beth. I am former drug addict. I hung out with the wrong people who smoke pot, inhale heroin."

Tears fell down her face. "Oh, God! We have a lot more in common."

"What! You did drugs too?"

"Hung out with the wrong people. I wasn't overweight either. I weighed 130, but after my roommate left California, I was lost. We used to listen to Hillsong and JesusCulture. I introduced her to soaking worship–"

"Soaking worship?"

"Beautiful Christian music you can soak or immerse in the same way when you bathe."

"Still, a strange concept."

"Not many people know of it. Soaking worship originated at the Toronto Airport Christian Fellowship."

"Do they teach that at your church?"

"My former church. My pastor was heavy into it. Have you heard of Graham Cooke?"

"Can't say I have."

She took out her cell phone and clicked on the YouTube app. "This is one of his sermons."

*****

Her heart soared as he enabled her to talk about a passion of hers—soaking worship. She had stopped soaking because her mom wasn't into it. When they moved, they attended another church. Her mom didn't want the memories of her late husband to resurface because her parents married there. Beth preferred incorporating soaking worship with a friend. If Stan showed interest, it would seal their relationship. She would continue her friendship with him.

"What do you think?"

"It's different."

"Do you think Larry would like it?"

"Probably not."

"I have a CD you can borrow if you want to listen to Julie True."

"I'll pray concerning it. Does your mother listen to soaking worship?"

"Sometimes. She works two four-hour jobs. She has lunch at home in between jobs."

"May I ask why you are living with her?"

The waitress arrived and thank goodness, too. "I'll have the Alaskan salmon special and a glass of iced tea."

"Brown rice or white rice?"

Beth never liked brown rice. She made a face. What would Stan think if she said white? Go for it! "White rice." She smiled.

She wrote down her order and regarded Stan. "And you?"

"The classic seafood salad and iced tea."

The waitress picked up the menus, then walked back to the rack.

He had such cute dimples when he smiled, and his eyes truly lit up. "You never answered my question."

She took a drink of her water. "I rented an apartment until I got involved with a man. He warned me of the dangers of living alone. He invited me to live with him, so he could protect me. I was gullible, Stan. I wanted someone to love me and he did…at least I thought he did. He abused me until a strong voice told me to flee. I couldn't return home, so I sought out my friend Julie."

"Where does Julie live? Where was Holly at that time?"

"Montana. Julie lived in California when she was hiding from her boyfriend. He found her, won her back, got married and now lives in Montana." Sharing her experiences made her thirsty and she finished her water. However, the waitress returned with their teas.

"Your meals should be ready in 15 minutes."

"Thank you," they both said.

"You're welcome." She left.

"Has Holly met Julie?"

"No. Why?"

"Just wondering."

"So, you found her in Montana and then what happened?"

"Rather not say."

"You don't have to tell me now."

"I like you, Stan. I'm not sure of myself. I had a couple of bad dates and well … I am a fat pig."

"No, don't say that.'

"Why not?"

"Because you're not."

"Why do you like me?"

"Because I understand you." He smiled, and said, "and you are beautiful."

"No man had said I was beautiful and meant it."

"They are not worthy of you. If you want to know, I had bad experiences with women, too, when I was obese."

Beth stared at her feet. "That's why you're working out?"

"I work out to keep in shape now. The weight loss took years. I felt the same way as you."

"Why don't you have a woman now?"

"I haven't met the right one."

"Years, huh?"

"Because I wasn't serious."

"At least you don't have a mother to hound you."

"Does she embarrass you?"

"Yes. People think something is wrong with me because I work out with my mother."

"Nonsense." He chuckled. "I did want to know what your story was."

"After my father died, I was all she had close by. I have an aunt in another town and my grandparents are alive, but they are in Florida."

"Beth, I was wondering. What do you think of my church? Would you attend again?"

"I better not. I don't want to give people the wrong impression."

"Okay. On Wednesday nights, we have a Fit for Life group. Would you come?"

As soon as he mentioned Fit for Life, it was like lightning striking her. She had seen that in the bulletin and wondered if he attended.

"You're welcome to join us."

Should she take a chance? She liked Stan, but she envisioned skinny people gawking at her and feeling sorry for her.

Go to it.

"Okay…as friends."

His smile widened. "The address is 319 West Palm, but I could take you with me."

People would think they came as a couple. They were friends. "I'll meet you there."

"All right."

Fifteen

Stan led Beth to her car. He didn't want their time to end and there was still light in the day. The lunch went a lot better than the first time they had lunch together.

He gazed at her, but she stared off into space. Her mind was miles away. "Penny for your thoughts."

"I don't want us to move too fast. We need to be careful."

There was an "us" in that statement. He liked that. "Neither do I. I wasn't going to kiss you."

"Well, that's nice." She giggled. "I do like you."

"Something else on your mind?" He lowered his voice.

"This feels like a date." She stared at the ground, then him. "I should get home."

He gave a weak smile, trying to hide his disappointment. "Okay."

"See you tomorrow?"

"Sure." He walked to his car, waving.

*****

Beth's heart broke. She had let him down. What was she supposed to do? Let him kiss her? He wanted to kiss her. "Didn't he want friendship?"

At the table, he asked about John. She couldn't help but detect a hint of jealousy. She never gave John the time of day. As far as she was concerned, she would rather have lunch with Stan and not John. To her, John represented the world and Stan, Jesus. "Angelique can have John."

Beth climbed into her Honda Accord and prayed, "God, am I doing the right thing? He doesn't look at my weight as the others do. He even understands. I have a feeling I'll see him more than I like. What do you think, God?"

The building off to the right, one she knew, drew her attention. Stan's church. The message the pastor preached was on thanking God for his provision, even if it was a little. A different take than what her pastor preached one time, but she liked the message. Still she felt self-conscious.

He's feeling sorry for you.

That wasn't from God and her blood pressure rose. "Get out, Satan!" She turned on her CD player on her dashboard and listened to Jesus Culture as she drove home.

"If he is for me, he will like Jesus Culture and Hillsong." He never said what or who he likes. He will tell her.

Upon arriving home, there was one car in the driveway. Her pastor must have left. She stepped out of her car and locked the doors.

Her mother watched her on the other side of the door. She smiled and waved to her. "How was your lunch?" her mother asked.

"He invited me to his Fit for Life group. The group meets on Wednesdays. Would you be okay if I go?" She didn't have to ask, but she wanted assurance.

"Sweetheart, yes, of course! Don't worry. Did you enjoy your lunch?"

"Yes, I did. He shared a little of his life with me. He also has a great sense of humor."

"This sounds like you might go out again." Her mother sounded hopeful.

"It's a possibility, but we aren't dating yet. Larry is seeing Holly."

"Hawthorne?"

"Yes, my friend from the country."

"I have news too. As you know," she said, leading her daughter in, "I asked the pastor to come over. I needed them to pray for me."

"Concerning?"

Her mother gave a knowing look and immediately she knew, and her heart raced. "Dad's death?"

"I miss him, sweetheart. Pastor Clint preached on letting go of grief. And the Lord spoke to me and told me it was time to move on." Tears fell down her face.

"Oh, mom!" She embraced her mother.

"And I am so sorry, I have been pushy towards you, treating you like my best friend. I need to let you be Beth. I'll try not to interfere in your life. If you don't want to see Stan–"

Beth put her finger to her lips. "I never said that, mom. Yes, you were pushy, but only a little and I needed that push."

"Sweetheart, do you mean that?" She wiped her eyes.

"Yes. I would be in my room feeling sorry for myself if you didn't insist."

Her mother wrapped her arms around Beth in embrace. "I love you, Beth. You and Jesus are all I have."

"Are we still on for tomorrow?"

"Yes!"

Sixteen

The members of Fit for Life weren't just made up of skinny people. While a couple were fit, the rest had weight issues and she had seen two members at the gym and she connected with Joann Stevenson, a 31-year-old single mom.

While she was at work, she prayed that John would not come in. She realized the enemy could have sent him. "Lord, I thank you for showing me that I have someone better than John."

"Not supposed to be praying at work," Angelique said.

Beth ignored her teasing reprimand. "I'll have you know I'm not interested in John. You can have him."

"I haven't seen him around." Angelique rung up a customer. "Is that all?"

"Yes, for now."

Beth continued shelving books as she whistled a tune.

"Can you stop that, please? I don't know why you Christians are always happy."

"We're happy because of Jesus."

"Yuck."

Beth giggled. She knew Angelique was against Christianity and her prejudice didn't bother her. She had learned to accept people like Angelique.

"Don't you know the world hates you people? Or do you care?"

"I throw my cares to the Lord." She smiled.

Angelique scratched her head, shaking it as she walked back to serving customers. She offered them cheery smiles and interacted with them.

Boys liked her. They would walk in and talk to her as they headed for the magazine section. Beth was once thin, and she mused that she will get there again.

*****

Stan waited a week to hear back from the missionary. His pastor said the call would take several months. Will they take that long to connect with him?

He tried to find satisfaction in his job. He would smile and greet customers as they entered the store and offer his help. He wasn't assigned to the cash register yet.

One day, he helped Lora and Lisa set up for a book signing. Author Meredith McConnell was going to make her presence known and sign her newest book, "County Fair Mystery." His pulse raced as they pushed a table to an empty area near the reading area.

"Do you read Meredith's books?" Lisa asked Stan.

They set the table down and Stan went to get the books they ordered from Meredith's publisher. A box of books with her name on it sat on the floor. He lifted the box and carried it out. "I'm not a big reader of mysteries," he responded to Lisa.

"What do you read? The Bible?" She knew he was a Christian.

He smiled. "Among other things."

Lisa took out the books and set them on the table. In less than an hour, Meredith would be here.

The book cover had a picture of a woman's face faded against the background. For some reason, he sensed that he had seen her before. Her eyes were daunting.

"Who is the woman on the cover?"

"You would have to ask Meredith, but she probably couldn't tell you either," Lora responded. "Why?"

"I've seen her before, I think."

"You have?"

"Looks vaguely familiar."

"Hmm."

Stan went back to his station, working in the coffee shop. Erica wasn't there today, and they assigned him to her place. "Someday I will have a job where I will not fill in for whoever is absent."

A short time later, a woman in a red dress and a red hat hurried in. He couldn't keep his eyes off Meredith. She was more stunning than the model on the cover. "Is my table ready? The train was late coming in," she complained. "Can't believe the slowness of public transportation."

"You're on time. Sorry about the readers outside. They are all eager to meet you," Lisa said, "including me. Can I be first since I have to work the register?"

Stan's ribs tickled him, and he suppressed a chuckle.

"What's your name, sweetheart?" Meredith made eye contact with Stan, whose mouth dropped open. "Do I know you? I think I went to school with you or something. What's your name, son?"

He pointed to himself. "Me?"

"You're the only man in here, aren't you?"

"Yes, ma'am. Stanley Powers."

"Stanley Powers! Well, how do you do? I used to be Meredith Matthews."

His heart raced, and his pulse quickened. "Yes! High school. You were my science partner! I haven't seen you in years!

"Fifteen long years, Stanley. Are you married? Seeing anyone?"

"No and yes. I have a friend I have been seeing."

"Male or female? I'm divorced. The man was a jerk. I should begin. Nice seeing you." And she smiled for the first time since she arrived.

Lisa walked up to him and hit him in the arm. "You didn't recognize her at first?"

"People change, you know that." He offered Lisa a genuine smile.

"She might be interested in you."

"I'm not interested in anyone."

"Touché." She walked back to the table

"What is your name again?" she asked Lisa.

"Lisa Bradford."

Meredith signed a book for her and gave it to her. "Stanley, after I do this, I would love to have lunch with you. The train doesn't leave until 1:30."

"Sure." He smiled.

Lisa's mouth dropped open. "Don't you have Beth?"

"Who's Beth?" Meredith asked.

"Stanley's girlfriend."

"We are friends, as Meredith and I are friends. I have my lunch break at 12."

"Perfect."

*****

John ambled into the Book Ends Bookstore and wandered around a section of books.

"Can I help you, John?" Beth walked over to his aisle.

"Just looking, Beth. I like your store."

"Aren't you working on a book?"

"Beth, why don't you like me?"

"I like you as a friend."

He stared past Beth. "Hi."

Beth acknowledged Jodi and said, "I'm helping him."

"Can I talk to you in private, Beth?"

"I hope you find what you are looking for."

"Me too." He smiled.

She followed Jodi to the back room. "What's up?"

"Are you flirting with the customer?"

She gasped. "Who told you I was flirting?"

"No one did. I saw how you were reacting to John."

"I wasn't flirting! I'm telling the truth. I was helping the customer."

Jodi smiled, but it was condescending. "Good. Flirting isn't in your job description."

Beth hadn't flirted with a customer since she worked for Roy and Loretta. Did Lisa call them as a reference? "I'll return to my station. I don't need the accusation."

As she shelved books, a still small voice said, *I have another for you.*

Stan. She had become friendlier to Stan as they had had a couple of lunches together and the occasional interactions at the gym. It brought a smile to her face. Since the time at Wendy's, he had helped her become comfortable around him.

However, she needed to work hard at losing weight. Weigh-in would be Saturday. She had watched what she had eaten, but a couple of times she allowed herself to have a cheeseburger from Burger World. She crossed her fingers, hoping she would have at least lost two pounds.

Seventeen

Stan parked his car outside Kelly's Diner, the diner closest to the train station. He glanced around and checked the time on his watch. Meredith told him to meet her here.

Why did he agree to meet her? The last he remembered, she was dating Conner Howard. Meredith wasn't popular, but people liked her. Stan was a football player and Meredith was his best friend's sister. He hadn't seen or heard anything since they graduated and now she is coming to have lunch with him.

Remember, I have someone else for you. Don't mislead her.

Beth. How could he forget Beth? The last time they had lunch together, she had become amicable toward him and she talked freely, especially when she shared her experience in Montana.

"I came to Montana to get away from Devon. I have lost touch with Julie. I didn't know where she lived until I remembered she was from Montana." She stopped there and sipped her tea. "But I had an ulterior motive after I met her husband. I was jealous. I led this man into the bookstore and he flirted with me. I thought he was interested in me until he saw Julie."

"Were you hurt?"

"Yes. Julie didn't need another man, I did! However, after I left the bookstore, he followed me and introduced himself to me. Said his name was Brad Melbourne." She stopped there and stared into space. "I thought I had ruined my friendship with Julie. Her husband never trusted me. I don't blame him because I flirted with him." She stared at her feet. "I didn't think Julie would forgive me, but she did."

She touched his heart with her honesty and willingness to share her story. He saw a future with her.

"Hello? Stan? Are you daydreaming?" Meredith took him out of his thoughts and he smiled up at her. "Meredith, I think I should be honest with you. I'm glad we reconnected, but God has someone else for me."

"Don't you worry, Stan. I'm not looking for a relationship. I just want to catch up."

He smiled as he opened his door. "All right."

Meredith led him inside the diner and they waited for a hostess to take them to a table. "Have you seen Jason lately?"

"I haven't seen him since he married Mary Beth and moved to Glendale."

"Two kids. I'm a lucky aunt."

He raised his eyebrows. "Lucky? I would say blessed."

She frowned. "When did you get religious?"

"Oh, after I had enough of doing drugs and alcohol. I had a friend who shared his faith with me. We share an apartment together."

"Hmm. I see. I married Keith right out of high school. Worst decision I've ever made."

"Oh?"

"How many in your party?" A waitress approached them.

"Two. We're each paying for our own lunch."

*****

Beth drove by Kelly's diner and her eyes lit up, but her heart raced. Stan dines here? His white Prius was in the parking lot. In the short time she has known him, he has never dined here.

As soon as a driver pulled out, she pulled in. She would surprise him. Maybe he was having lunch with Larry. Stan had told her when he dines alone, he would use a fast-food drive through and order a salad.

Don't be deceived.

Why? As she entered the restaurant, a woman in a red outfit was talking to Stan. Who was the woman? If Stan could have lunch with a stranger, then why couldn't she have one with John? Her blood boiled, but she calmed down.

She headed towards his table. "Hi!"

"Beth, hi! Meet Meredith. We went to high school together and she is an author."

"Interesting. Is she single?"

"Divorced, why?" Stan was puzzled by her blunt question, and he gazed at her, a bit dumbfounded.

"Oh nothing. Nice to meet you, Meredith." And she ran out. God told her not to be deceived, but how could she not feel like she had been? Meredith was thin! Tears streamed down her face. "Why I am so jealous? We're friends." She climbed into her car and put in a Jesus Culture CD. She blew out some air. "Oh, God!"

Beth, why are you so upset?

She wiped her tears. "I'm undeserving. He is probably more attracted to her than me."

"And how do you know that?"

Her pulse quickened. God didn't say that! She stared out her window, and Stan was smiling down at her. Thickness gathered in her throat and she wanted to hide somewhere. She expected Stan to be angry, but his smile said forgiveness. I'm undeserving of him.

Listen to him.

Beth opened the door and he sat in the passenger seat. She said nothing. God said to listen.

"I told her that God has someone else for me."

A jolt went through her body. If that was so, then why was he having lunch with her? Did she care? "I'm sorry. I overreacted."

"I haven't seen her since graduation. She was my best friend's sister."

"Did…you date her?"

"No. She was dating a jock name Conner. He played football with me."

"You played football?"

He chuckled. "Yes, but I didn't play in college."

A smile crept up on her sad face. No wonder he had muscles on him. He didn't gain muscles from working out? Or did he? "You're not interested in her?"

"Nope." His eyes showed love. "I'm touched, Beth. I thought we were just friends, but you acted like a jealous lover."

She giggled. "I know. Silly me. As I said, I'm sorry."

"She happened to have a book signing at the bookstore where I work."

"What's her last name? Maybe I heard of her."

"Meredith McConnell."

Her skin tingled. "County Fair Mystery?"

"So, you have."

"I love mysteries. I wish I would have known. I would have asked for her autograph. And I would not have acted like that."

"Do you feel better now?" His smile warmed her heart.

"Much, but I am embarrassed."

"Don't be. To be honest," he chuckled, "I get jealous when you are talking with John.

"Thinking of him, my supervisor accused me of flirting with him." She giggled. "Here I am a 187-pound woman flirting with a handsome author. Yeah right. When pigs fly.

Both laughed.

Stan gasped. "Look! A flying pig!"

"Oh, shut up!" She gave him a playful punch.

"You are a beautiful 187-pound woman and I am serious." Stan had the bluest eyes she had ever seen. She felt drawn to his lips and soon they met in a passionate embrace… until she pulled away.

"Too soon."

"I don't think so." He touched her face. "I think God is for us."

"But how can you love a pig?"

"Stop calling yourself a pig."

"I'm a–"

"Beautiful woman. God would agree."

Tears trickled down her face. She had struggled with her self-esteem, but God had sent her an angel in the form of a man who was once overweight himself. Quite handsome too. She smiled to him. “Thank you.”

“You’re more than welcome.” He checked the time on his watch. “Wow! Look at the time! I better get back to work. See you tomorrow morning?”

“Yes.”

Stan reached to kiss her cheek, then climbed out and walked to his car.

Beth touched the place where he kissed her and held her hand there. “Thank you, God.”

Eighteen

"Wow, Beth! Look at you! You're all aglow!" Jodi's eyes were agape as Beth walked in.

Beth's cheeks felt warm too. "I found a man who could love me for me."

"John?" Jodi teased.

"No. Angelique can have him if he is interested in her. Stan. Stan was having lunch with a woman and I got jealous for no reason."

"And you are glowing because of it?"

"No, of course not, but he wasn't mad at me when I ran out on him."

"If he is seeing another woman, that's a red flag."

"He's not seeing another woman. She's a woman from his high school days. She was his best friend's sister."

"Guard your heart. If he is willing to have lunch with a woman behind your back, he will cheat on you."

Jodi couldn't take her feeling of euphoria away. Stan is not a cheater. She eyed Angelique behind the cash register; she had a decided smirk on her face. *I need a better job.*

Suddenly, a long-dormant desire emerged from her heart. A desire she had when she was thin. She wanted a family and she could see it with Stan. Their lips would have met. What would have happened if she had allowed him to kiss her? Did he have self-control? Could he stop himself? She didn't know him well enough, but she wanted to get healthy for Stan.

*****

He walked in to his workplace with his face uplifted and smiled to all the staff. “Hello, everyone!”

“Did you and Meredith connect with each other?” Lisa asked.

“No.” His hands tingled. His limbs lightened. “But I’m on top of the world.”

“What happened? I’ve never seen you like this!” Lisa exclaimed.

“What happened was Beth. It was in her eyes. We were going to kiss, but she said it was too soon.”

Lisa’s face was scrunched up in a rather disapproving expression. “How did she get in the picture?”

He walked toward the backroom. He stopped to face Lisa. “She saw a woman having lunch with me. If she didn’t care, it would have been a no big deal, but it was.” He continued onto the back room for his assignment.

“Wait! She was jealous?” Lisa followed him in.

“Who was jealous?” Lora asked, sitting behind her desk.

“Beth. She assumed I had another woman in my life and ran out. That tells me–”

“She can’t compete?” Lisa asked.

“She hoped for a relationship with me, as I would like one with her.”

Lisa stole a look from Lora and shot it at Stan. “Oh.”

“What did I miss?”

“We thought this lunch date would lead to something else.”

“Didn’t you know about my friendship with Beth?”

"Friendship, but not romance," Lora said.

"Friendship leads to romance. I would have kissed her if she didn't pull away."

"The lady is afraid to kiss."

The sound of pages ruffling got louder, and he could feel his body temperature rising. Narrowing his eyes, he stared at Lisa. "Why are you against Beth? What has she done to you?" He glared at her sharply.

'Nothing, but the way you describe her, she sounds as if she has low self-esteem. Listen, you don't want a woman who gets easily jealous and clingy. Meredith would be better for you."

"You judge by appearance, but I judge the heart and she has a good one." With that, he checked his timesheet and went to his station. *Another 4 hours and I go home.*

Inside her house, Beth collapsed. She never thought she'd face persecution from Jodi. Wasn't Jodi in her corner? Yet both women wouldn't leave her alone about Stan. "Why is everyone against me seeing Stan?"

"Stan?" Her mother rushed out of her room. She gasped when she saw Beth on the floor. "What happened?" She wiped the tears from her daughter's eyes.

"They think Stan is no good for me." More tears ran down her cheeks. Beth tried to tell her mother what happened since lunch time. "He told me I was beautiful, and they want to take it away from me." She cried on her mother's shoulders.

"Honey, don't listen to them. They don't have your best interests in mind, but God does. What has He told you?"

"A couple of things. First, He said He has someone else besides John for me. Then later, as Stan's car was outside Kelly's Diner, God told me not to be deceived, but I went in and saw him with a woman. He told me they were high school friends." Her frown faded into a smile. "I overreacted and left the diner…Mom, he said I'm beautiful and we would have kissed, but I was scared."

"Oh, sweetheart! That is great! You both are having feelings for each other."

Beth's limbs lightened. She suddenly buoyant and strong. "No man has ever made me feel this way. You know I expected him to react in anger but instead…. he showed love." She covered her mouth.

"He loves you!"

More tears fell but they were happy tears. "And that's when Satan reared his ugly butt in my face, trying to get me to doubt Stan's love for me."

"Satan doesn't want you happy. Are you going to see Stan again?"

She nodded. "You bet!" She let her mom pull her up, even as heavy as she was. "One thing is clear, and I intend to lose weight before I get married."

"Now, you're talking."

"Will you help me? And thanks for getting me started… and uh…embarrassing me at the gym!" She giggled as she went to her room.

"You're welcome. By the way, Julie called. Wanted to know if you're free Saturday."

Beth stopped midstride, her skin tingling. "She called here?"

"Yes. She tried to get a hold of you on your cell phone."

"I had it off. I didn't want distractions. I'll call her back."

"All right. We're having Lean Cuisines today."

"Sounds good." She headed for her room, which was upstairs. A she entered her room, she felt light and her heart was full. She had so much to thank God for and she wanted to stop and take in His goodness.

She collapsed on her bed, but because she was tired. Her day was long, but good. She took her cell phone out of her pocket and checked her voicemails.

****

Stan arrived at his apartment. He had had a long day, but he made it through without hearing Lisa and Lori trying to talk him out of seeing Beth. "Tomorrow, I am going to invite her to a concert at Newport." He walked in and headed for the kitchen. Larry was not around. Knowing his friend and roommate, he was probably seeing Holly. Funny how two confirmed bachelors each had a woman to unconfirm it. The day before he met Beth, he prayed God would send a woman Larry's way, but instead, God used Larry to encourage Stan to be her friend. But if Beth wasn't friends with Holly, Larry would be undateable.

The front door opened, then slammed shut. Sounded like Larry was angry. He came out and Larry had a sullen face. "What's up?"

"Holly was with someone else."

"What? What are you saying?"

"She went back to her ex." He stormed into his room. "I thought she liked me, but she said her heart was for Clint."

"Ouch."

"So, I am a confirmed bachelor again."

There went that theory.

Stan followed him into his room where Larry took off his boots. "How is it going with Beth?"

Stan sat beside him. "Better than I thought."

"Good. I'm glad to hear. You hungry?"

"Always."

"Sloppy Joes okay with you?"

"Fine with me. I just need to rest. Call me when you're ready."

"I will." He left his room. "I guess you don't have to go back to farming."

"Just as well."

Nineteen

They hadn't been friends for a long time, but on one of their dates, they picnicked under the stars at Liberty Park. Beth's palms were sweaty, and her stomach fluttered. She didn't expect a proposal, but she hoped he would ask her if she was ready to date as boyfriend and girlfriend. Her heart pounded.

Stan took a drink of his bottled water. "I love your eyes. They are like green emeralds."

"I thought they were close to olive green."

"You say olive, I say emerald."

"Okay." She blushed. She was used to his kind words and she blushed.

"You look great. How many pounds have you lost?"

"Twelve."

"Twelve in six weeks! All because you and your mom went on a weight-loss plan?"

She smiled. "I'm not doing it for me, but for us." She took a drink of her wine. His face shined. "You make me love you more."

Beth smiled. Her heart continued to pound. He was going to ask her. Julie told her how Eric had ruined it for them, but nothing could ruin this day unless this news was about the next step.

"Would you be okay if I went to Greece?"

What? She set down her can of diet soda, her body heat rising. Before, she didn't care if he went to Greece. She forgot he planned to leave for Greece, but now? "So soon? I thought you said it would take months!"

"Yes, it will. I met with the missionaries. I just need to get funds from churches, learn the language, get my passport and get myself acquainted with what's involved. How would you feel if I was gone?"

His question left a bad taste in her mouth. Did she still want him to go? After praying, peace washed over her. "Maybe by the time you get back, I'll be thin for you." She offered a weak smile, but she ached inside.

"Things may progress between us and by the time I am ready, you'll be my wife."

She spat out what she had in her mouth. "Progress? I thought– Oh God! Is this what the dinner date is about?"

"Beth, I love you. I want to know if you are secure in my love for you. After what happened last month–"

Her temperature went up. "You are bringing last month up?"

"I don't want you to think I will fall in love with a Greek, when I have you. I told you I love you."

"Is it love to bring up something you wish to forget?"

"Beth, I don't want to forget. That was the day, at least in my mind that I think we truly discovered each other and I don't hold it against you either." He reached for her hand.

Her mouth dropped open. She had no words. This man was simply amazing. Full of love and understanding. She never had a relationship like this.

"You're also not a fat pig." He wiped away her tears. "Beth, I think we are ready for a relationship. I want to know if you will be true to me while I'm gone, but I also want to know that if we marry before I become a missionary, you will go with me."

She nodded as more tears cascaded down her face. "Yes. And Yes."

"Because if we are to go steady, there can't be room for anyone else. Do you love me?"

"Without a doubt."

"You made me happy. Thank you, Beth." He reached to kiss her, and she returned the kiss.

She wanted to say there wouldn't be anyone else who would want her. Although she liked John, she never had believed he was the one. "My view of you and John is you two are opposite of each other. He represents the world and you represent Christ, so yes, I chose you."

He smiled wide. "Do you enjoy walks? Maybe after dinner, we can walk together."

"I would love to."

After they enjoyed their picnic, they cleaned up and packed up their basket. Beth wanted to enjoy the moment. He said he loved her. She was convinced of it. When he mentioned her running out on him, she fought back angry tears. However, he said it in a good way. He mentioned the incident with love. No condemnation.

It won't last. He will grow tired of you and move onto someone else.

Beth refused to entertain negative thoughts and she pushed it away as she waited for Stanley to put the basket in his car. "Get lost, Satan!"

"Ready?" he asked, returning to her, and grabbed her hand.

She felt a tingling sensation and she smiled. “Yes.”

The air was cool, and Beth shivered as they walked. Stan removed his cardigan and wrapped her with it “Better?”

She nodded. “Thank you, Stanley.”

“You’re welcome.” He held her close.

Stan walked with an upturned face. All was well in his world. Beth was in his arms, and there would be no one to tear them apart. Even while he would be in Greece, he knew Beth would be at home waiting for him. No, better yet, they could start a family in Greece. They would marry before his church sends him to Greece.

Beth had compared him to Jesus. What an honor. Although he thought Beth would go after John, he left her in God’s hands. *God, you’re awesome!* John became a Christian months ago and Beth needed someone strong in his faith. He worried if she had chosen him, she would still struggle with her insecurities. God had not sent John to her, but him.

Beth stared off into space with a smile on her face. Her eyes sparkled in the moonlight. She was radiant like the sun. She had come a long way from that insecure woman she was at the gym. She glowed. “Do you want a family?”

“Yes, I do.” His smile spoke volumes.

“Me too. I love kids.

Do you have any siblings?”

“Two brothers. And you?” he asked, looking at her.

“Only child.”

“Your parents must have pampered you.”

"Only my mom."

"How is Holly?"

"I guess you know that it didn't work out with Holly and Larry."

"Yeah. He came home quite upset."

"Clint begged Holly to come back to him"

"I see."

"I love you," she said.

"I love you too."

She kissed him. "I had a lovely night."

"I as well."

The moon shined down on them and radiated the inner beauty of Beth, his girlfriend. He loved the sound of that word - girlfriend. He had to wait on the Lord's timing. It was worth the wait. Beth was all that he wanted in a woman. Being with her sufficed.

She breathed in and out, but her breaths were slow and easy. "The moon is gorgeous tonight. God is so good, isn't He?" She closed her eyes.

"Yes, He is. Have you ever imagined dating me before tonight?" Her eyes were as lovely as emeralds.

She turned her attention to him. "Not a month ago. For some reason, I didn't care for you, but I guess God was telling me, though I wasn't picking up on it right away, that you are the one He has for me. We have so much in common."

"Beth, I believe you can lose all that weight. I know you can."

"I know. I had to give up a lot food I enjoyed eating. Grateful for my mom." She grabbed his hand, which created a spark.

He grinned. "Did you feel that?"

"Yes."

"I guess we have chemistry."

For a while, they gazed at each other, not saying a word. It was okay. He was content in her presence.

The moment was perfect for Beth. She was his and as far as she was concerned, there were no others. She smiled with an upturned face. "I wish we could stay like this forever."

He checked the time on his watch. "We do have church service tomorrow. Would you do me the honor of attending the service with me?"

She gazed into his blue eyes. A month ago, she wanted to check the church out. She attended once, but since he'd asked her to be his girlfriend, she was at ease with him. "What time should I be ready?"

"8:30."

"Okay then."

He planted a kiss on her cheek, then walked to his car. "See you tomorrow!" he called out.

Beth felt giddy, like a teenager. It has been a long time since she felt loved. He didn't view her as a fat pig; he saw her as beautiful.

Beth unlocked her car door and climbed in. She turned on her radio to Mercy Me's **Beautiful**. Confirmation from God that what Stan said was true. "Thank you, Jesus.

Twenty

The following day, Stan straightened his bow tie. The mirror showed him smiling.

"Are you impressing God or Beth?" Larry teased as he watched Stan with his tie.

"I don't need to impress God." Stan stared at his friend. "You and I need to talk." He frowned.

"What's up?" Larry was oblivious to why the need to talk.

"What really happened between you and Holly? I thought you liked her."

"I do, but she prefers Clint. So, I left."

"Did she actually tell you that?"

Larry sighed heavily and narrowed his eyes. "Do we have to discuss Holly and me?"

Stan fixed the cufflinks on his dress shirt. They should discuss the matter, but Larry showed annoyance to his question. However, he didn't want to put him in a bad mood before church. "I need to pick up Beth. Will you be at the service?" He smiled.

"Yeah, I will. Glad it's working out for you and Beth."

Stan chuckled. "Funny how we weren't looking. See you later." He picked up his Bible and headed for his car.

Butterflies made themselves known as Beth applied eye shadow to her eyes. Her first time accompanying Stan to his church. Last week, he took her to a concert at Newport and it was Hillsong! Her heart soared when he showed her the ticket last week.

"I remembered Hillsong is one of your favorite groups. I wanted to surprise you. Are you surprised?" He escorted her into the church building.

"Yes! I knew they were going to perform but didn't know anyone would attend with me. This means more."

"I'm glad. I also…um… listened to a couple songs by Julie True."

"And?" She held her breath. If he sayshe likes her, he's a keeper.

"She has a lovely voice, but your voice is lovelier."

He practically took her breath away and her heart melted. "You never heard me sing!"

"I have when you're in my car and one time when you visited the place I worship at." He smiled as he brushed strands of her hair from her face. "You have a beautiful voice."

Beth felt heat in her cheeks. "Thanks. So, do you like Julie True?"

He didn't respond. Did that mean no? Stan stared past her, into the distance, as if he was thinking. "Does it matter if I like her or not?"

He didn't. What was it with men and soaking worship music? As Beth pondered the question, it occurred that men generally aren't as intimate as women are. "How do you relax?"

"Recline in my chair." His smile warmed her heart.

"Okay." Did it matter? It would have been nice if he enjoyed Julie as she did, but he was good to her. Could she compromise? Eric wasn't either, but it didn't stop Julie from loving Eric. "Would you allow it in our home?"

"Yes."

At his answer, her heart soared, and her face lifted up. "If you had said no, I would have had to break up with you."

"You're welcome, Beth." He kissed her cheek.

The doorbell rang, which took her out of memory lane.

"Stan's here!" Her mother announced.

Beth finished applying the pink lipstick, and she sprayed a little cologne on her neck.

"Wow! I have never seen you so lovely!!" Her mother came in.

Heat radiated in her cheeks. "Thanks."

"You look great in your floral dress."

"Thanks, mom. You are beautiful as well." She had on a white blouse with a laced trim and a light pink skirt, but her mom always wore skirts to their place of worship. "Is your boyfriend picking you up?"

"I'm meeting him at his church."

"His church?" She turned to her mom. "So, it's serious?"

"Not that serious, sweetie. He invited me, but I told him I'd meet him there."

Her mom took her breath away. They were so much alike! Although Ann didn't have a long way to go as she did, they both took the same approach to dating. Shortly after her mom met Howard, she attended his church. She wanted to decide whether to see him or not. The city had four charismatic churches. The one they attended was within city limits while another was out near the highway. The other two had small congregations. Did Howard attend a charismatic church? "Is he charismatic?"

Her mom sighed. "No. You better get down there before Stan wonders."

Stan checked his watch. How long did it take Beth to finish up? He had been waiting ten minutes? It was 3 minutes until 8:30. "Beth!"

"Coming!"

His heart raced as Beth walked down the stairs in a graceful manner. "Wow! You look radiant!"

She blushed. "You're handsome."

He took her hand as she neared the bottom of the stairs. "Nice place you have here. How long have you lived here?"

Twelve years," Ann replied.

"We better get going," Stan said. He led Beth to his car. He opened the door and waited for her to get in.

"Sorry I held us up."

"Can I ask what happened?"

"Nerves." She reached for his hand, although he had them on the wheel. She wanted assurance he wasn't mad. "Then my mom came."

"Ahh." He smiled. "Your first time attending as my girlfriend."

Her cheeks reddened. "I'm still insecure, but I'm a lot thinner than I was last month."

"Is the Fit for Life helping you accept your identity in Christ?"

"It helps to know others have the same issue." She gazed at him. "You helped too." She took her hand off him, then adjusted her seatbelt.

They arrived shortly before 8:30 and Stan's skin tingled. God got them there on time. He smiled to Beth. "Ready?"

She smiled in return.

He climbed out of his car and walked to the other side, to help her out. After locking up, he took her hand and led her to his class.

"You made it!" Larry startled Beth, and she had to catch her breath. "Sorry about that."

"Just in time too," Stan responded. He led Beth to a couple of empty chairs.

"I forgive you." Beth took the seat Stan pulled out for her.

"Stan, is something going on between you two?" the teacher asked.

"Hi, Beth! Haven't seen you in a while," said a grinning young lady.

"Hi. And you are?"

"Jolene, but you can call me Jolie for short."

Jolene must be close to her age, she thought. She was overweight, and it made her smile. She could like her. "Nice to meet you." She sat in a chair.

"We are starting a new series on the Fruits of the Spirits. You should have in front of you a printout, which is an expository on Ephesians 5:21 and 22," the teacher began.

Beth's heart pounded as she opened her Bible to Ephesians 5. At her place of worship, her teacher started a new subject, one that didn't interest her—The Coming of the Lord. She had questioned the use of the scripture. They weren't that close to His coming. As a result, she stopped attending Bible study. What subject were they studying now? It won't matter after she becomes a member of Stan's church. Is this the day? She glanced over at Stan. His smile said I love you.

You are making him happy.

She shined like the sun. His heart palpitated. What was she thinking? Wouldn't it be great if she would become a member of the church? He prayed. Lord, let it be today.

When she visited last month, his heart shrunk because she didn't return. He had asked the Lord to show him a sign she was the one, but the Lord declined. He had to walk by faith. Stanley accepted and here she was today. Would she become a member? He cleared his throat.

On the way to the sanctuary, Beth let him hold her hand. He loved the feel of her skin on his. When their hands met, it sparked.

Beth smiled with an upturned face. "I've been thinking."

Here it comes.

"I love your church, and I love the sermons. Lately, I've been unhappy at mine and I think mom wants to switch churches." She cleared her throat. "Everyone here is so nice." She gazed at him. He sensed it coming.

"They are friendly."

"I would like to attend on a regular basis…"

He tried to keep his heart from shrinking, but his smile slipped. "Okay."

"…as a member."

His stomach fluttered, and he lost his breath. "As a member?"

"Surprised?"

"Not that I don't want you to be, but you heard one message." He could have kicked himself in his head for saying that. Don't discourage her. You wanted this! "I'm sorry. I shouldn't have said that."

Before they arrived at the lobby, she stopped and gazed at him. "I feel secure in your love. I know I have heard only one message, but I have a feeling God will bless me here." She touched his face.

"Beth Miller. I love you. Let me escort you inside." He stared at her.

"You may!"

His hands tingled as he held her hand and she giggled. As he led her into the lobby, he thought nothing could ruin the day. Once she becomes a member, she could even join him in Greece! Wouldn't that be wonderful?

Everyone smiled as they accepted a worship guide from Greg. Stan led Beth inside.

"Where do you want to sit?"

Beth prayed the previous night that Holly and Larry would reunite. She scanned the room, hoping to see them.

Stan didn't mention anything about Larry and Holly. Larry sat toward the front, but no Holly. Today she wouldn't mind sitting next to Stan. He had become more of her type. *God looks at the heart and so should I.*

She smiled. She knew where to sit. "Let's join Larry. Is that okay?"

His eyes widened. "Are you sure? He's close to the front."

"He's in the third pew from the front."

"Alrighty then!" With an uplifted face, he escorted her toward the third pew and, not wanting her to be sandwiched by two guys, he slid in and then helped her inside.

She raised her eyebrows. "Are you afraid he'll bite?"

"I thought you'd be more comfortable being on the outside."

"Are your possessive of me?"

"Nope. I know who you love."

"I appreciate the thoughtfulness." She cuddled next to him.

Stan leaned over to Larry and whispered something to him. "Are you keeping secrets from me?" she asked.

"I was informing him of what you told me."

Larry smiled. "You made a good choice, Beth. Pastor Andrews is awesome!"

"I'm sure he is."

Beth waited. She worshipped, listened to the sermon and when the pastor gave the altar call, she scooted out of the pew. Her heart raced, but her skin tingled as she made her way to the front. She approached the pastor.

Joyful tears ran down Stan's face. Beth whispered to his pastor what she decided. *Thank you, God! Thank you, Jesus!*

His pastor held his arm around her. A few people came up for prayer. He had her sit on a pew, then he attended to a member who was on his knees.

Beth smiled as she glanced back at Stan and he returned a wide one. "I love you," he whispered.

God told him to walk by faith and he did. Beth would now become a member of the church. Tears pour down his face

"I've never seen you this way before. She is a keeper, isn't she?" Larry asked, bringing him out of his introspection.

Stan nodded. "Yes, sir!"

Twenty-one

After service, as people welcomed her to the congregation, someone touched Stan as on his shoulder.

"Stan Powers?" The voice came from a deacon.

His eyes raised when he recognized Bob Crandon. "What's up?"

"The pastor wanted me to tell you to meet him in his office."

The pastor sent Bob to tell him, but he didn't remember them talking "What is it about?"

"He'll tell you." He smiled. "Nice to have your girlfriend joining us." He walked away.

There was a chill in the air, but the air conditioner was off. He offered a prayer to the Lord, asking for peace. Odd, the pastor wanted to meet with him. Why? Had he done something wrong? He hadn't sinned, had he? He felt no conviction in his heart. Stan shook his head as he walked to the office.

Bob wouldn't have a motive to tell a lie or set a trap. Stan envisioned his girlfriend coming in with him. Would he tell her first? "Lord, I have kept a clean life. I have been drug-free for five years and I have had no alcohol. So, what's up?"

"Nothing, son." The pastor arrived unannounced. "I called you concerning Greece." He sat behind his desk. "Plans have changed."

"Beg your pardon?" He kept his anger under control. He glanced around. Beth didn't come in with him. "You told her to wait outside?"

"Last night, the missionary couple called. They tried to get a hold of you, but you weren't home, or your cell was off."

He lowered his head in shame, but he regarded his pastor. "I wanted an uninterrupted night with Beth."

"I respect that. I didn't know Beth wanted to become a member and they don't know who she is or have any knowledge of her. It had nothing to do with her."

Beth waited outside the church office. She greeted everyone with a smile. "Welcome, Beth. I'm deacon Bob."

"Hi! What's going on in the office? He seemed serious when he told me to wait outside."

Bob looked her over and offered a friendly smile. "Not for me to say. Are you aware Stan could ask you to join him?"

"Join him where?"

"Greece or wherever he goes."

"I know about Greece. I hope—no! They're discussing Greece?"

"I don't know. I wouldn't worry though."

"Beth." Larry called.

She glanced at him. "What's up, Larry?"

"I have a question for you."

"All right. Thanks for letting me know, pastor." Stan walked out, sounding disappointed. "Let's talk in the car, Beth."

Her pulse quickened, and her stomach rolled. By the way he spoke, it didn't sound good. In a gentle voice, she asked, "bad news?"

He pressed his lips. "Yes." He led her to his car and helped her in.

After buckling her seat belt, she stared at her lap. She couldn't be the problem, could she? I didn't have an ulterior motive for joining his church.

"The couple bailed out on me." He climbed in and fastened his seat belt. "So, the pastor suggested a couple other countries that needs missionaries." He touched her leg near him. "Not your fault."

"It wasn't because I'm not married to you?"

"They don't know about you."

"Why did they bail out on you? Wouldn't they want you to join them?"

"Someone from a sister church put in a request. It's called preference."

She straightened up and put on her best face. "We will serve elsewhere."

He shot her a look and his mouth fell open. "Did you say we? What if we end up in a small African nation?"

"Isaiah responded to God's call, 'Here I am! Send me!' If God called, you to go to Africa–"

"I thought he called me to Greece. I had my heart set on Greece."

"Then we need to pray and ask God for directions."

His heart felt full and heat radiated in his chest. God had given him a treasure. “Beth Miller, I love you!” He reached to kiss her cheek. “Where do you want to have lunch? We should celebrate you becoming a member.”

She blushed. “I love you too. A Fresh Start? Seems like a Sunday tradition.”

He chuckled. “It sure does. A Fresh Start it is.” He turned on the radio and started the engine.

The woman next to him made his heart freeze, then it pounded. Her faith was astounding. He thanked God for sending him Beth and he smiled.

“God will work it out. His call and gifts are irrevocable.”

“Yes, He will. Thanks for the reminder.”

A song by Hillsong played on the radio and she gasped. “What a perfect song!”

“Still?”

“Yes. A reminder that God is still on His throne, and He will work out his plans for us.”

Amazing! His heart raced, and a wide grin appeared on his face. “Yes, He most certainly is!”

“I talked to Larry while you were in the office.” She stared at her feet.

“About Holly?”

“Yes. I wanted to hear for myself. I doubt Holly would lie to me.”

He nodded. Larry wouldn’t hide the truth from him, would he? Although Larry was as much a man of God as he was, he was human like any man on earth. He knew what was in a man's heart because he was one. He kept his voice low. "What did he tell you?"

"Same thing he told you. I got mad and called him a liar." She folded her arms.

"Wow! You're the first!"

"Holly is more hurt than he is. Clint left her for another woman and her father is ill. She is going through depression.

"And whammo! He's not interested." He frowned. He could give him a good talking to, but it was between Larry and the Lord. He would have to pray for him. *God, if I could open my heart to let a woman in, then so can Larry. Help him see that.*

On the other hand, Larry didn't want to leave city life and Holly wasn't right for him. He shook his head. No, Larry was stubborn. What if God was calling him and Larry ignored Him. He scratched his head. Wait! Larry told Beth the same thing? He shot her a look. "Did he just flat out tell you Holly lied to you?"

"Something like that."

"Hmm."

*****

The line at A Fresh Start was long. Stan checked the time on his watch. "We can eat at another restaurant," Beth suggested.

"Wonder why today? Larry and I dine here every Sunday afternoon."

"Someone's having a birthday, maybe. Thinking of that, when is yours?"

"Same month as yours, remember?" He scanned the room and his eye caught a glimpse of colorful balloons. "Why would someone have a kid's birthday here?"

"Not that this place is just for adults." She didn't care for this place before she dieted. Heat radiated in her cheeks. Her heart filled as she remembered seeing Stan here with Larry.

"I've never seen you glow like that."

"Just grateful."

"Yoo-hoo, Beth!"

Hearing her mother's voice caused her to skin to tingle. She searched for the source of the voice and someone waved to her from the front of the line. "Mom!"

Stan shifted his attention toward the front. "Hello, Ms. Miller." He smiled.

"So good to see you two together! We'll save you a table!" Her voice was buoyant and cheery.

Stan glanced toward the couple, then at Beth. "Your mom's new boyfriend?"

All her limbs tingled, and she felt overcome with emotion. God not only provided a man for her mom but for her as well. She had seen less of her mom because Ann's boyfriend would take her out several times a week. Beth would have the house to herself and she'd used the opportunity to play Julie True CDs on the stereo in the front room. Wonderful times spent with the Lord. Now if only she could get Stan to like Julie True. . "Yes. He's been wonderful to her. She attends his church now."

He eyed Beth. "Oh?" He smiled.

"Both of us were sensing God wanted to have us leave the place we attend service. Maybe He was preparing us for you men." She giggled.

"How is everything at work?"

"The same. John hasn't been coming by. Probably busy writing a book."

"Okay."

"And Angelique?"

"The same as usual, snarky, but I still pray for her."

"My coworkers are the same too. They razz me about you, but they stopped bugging me concerning Meredith."

Beth giggled. "Funny, how our coworkers bug us about an author. Jodi thinks I should go after John." She glanced at Stan. "If I wasn't so insecure about my weight, I might have."

"You would? Seriously?"

"He's quite handsome. Reminds me of Liam Neeson."

"The actor from Star Wars Episode 1?" Stan grinned.

"I'm a huge Star Wars fan. I haven't seen the old ones though."

The line moved, and they were closer to the front. Beth prayed. They could have gone to Sizzler's or Olive Garden, but A Fresh Start had become their Sunday restaurant. Stan and Larry liked it too. She scanned the room for Larry. She told him to give Holly another chance. She had said to Larry, "You were the spring in her step." Maybe Larry needed to get over his past hurts.

"What did you think of the sermon?"

"The sermon? It interested me, and I liked it." She smiled.

Beth's mind seemed a million miles away. Was she thinking about the sermon? The pastor preached about finding their worth in Christ. Beth had struggled with hers, but during the past weeks, she had gradually changed before him, turning into a beautiful flower.

Or was she thinking about the news? She'd displayed great faith. His heart froze, then pounded. Or something else? Did she want to go to Greece? *Lord, didn't you call me to go to Greece?* He lifted his eyes to heaven.

Didn't I tell you to have faith?

Stan grinned. "Yes, sir!"

Beth giggled. "Having a private convo with God?"

"About Greece," he admitted.

"God will work it out." She moved up.

"Almost there."

Before eating, they asked the Lord to bless the food. A tradition since their first date. Beth enjoyed their dates. Long walks along the beach, holding hands and going to movies. She closed her eyes.

"Praying?"

"Thanking God and being grateful."

"So am I."

After their meal, he asked if she would enjoy a drive with him. She declined, explaining, "I haven't seen my mom and I would love to spend time in worship."

"Ahh, all right. I'll see you at the gym."

Her mother was staring out the window, probably watching for her. Beth saved up to live elsewhere, but she would miss her mother. *I need to loosen myself from her.*

"Have you saved up for an apartment? How much are you making a month? I know it's not my business–"

"You must be reading my mind."

He chuckled. "She's waiting for you?"

Beth lost herself in his blue eyes. "I had a nice time and enjoyed the service. I'll attend next week, of course."

"Of course. I love you. See you tomorrow."

The moment was right. Her pulse raced. Her legs weakened. "I hate to leave."

"I offered to take us for a drive. The offer is still open." He touched her face.

She wished he would propose officially. He had, after all, spoken of marriage as if it was their ultimate destiny. She wanted more time with Stan, but God was calling her to spend time with Him at the moment. She needed her time with the Lord. She checked the time on her watch. "Wow! Two o'clock?"

He chuckled. "We spent an hour at the restaurant."

"Seems like it."

"Lunch at Wendy's tomorrow."

"Sounds good unless mom has other plans."

"Spend time with Jesus. I'll see you tomorrow."

She giggled, but inside her heart saddened. She wished he would like soaking worship too. But her heart saddened because he didn't kiss her. "Okay."

Before she stepped out, he reached over and kissed her cheeks. Her skin tingled. "I didn't expect the kiss." She smiled.

He chuckled. "Sorry I delayed it. Just thinking."

"Oh." She felt the tension leave. "Bye." She stepped out.

*****

As she headed for her house, a tear trickled down his face. He wished he could do more for Beth; he had wanted to kiss her lips. Why couldn't he? He hoped she wasn't disappointed.

They hadn't been dating for long and she was looking more beautiful by the day. He didn't want the day to end, but he loved her heart. "Lord, would she come with me if we end up going to Africa?"

Again, the Lord chided him. *Where is your faith*?"

He didn't have as much faith as Beth. She amazed him! Was she relieved, or did she have great faith?

A woman waved to him from the door. Why doesn't her mother invite him in? He smiled and waved back.

I need to pray, he thought. His mind was on Beth but not the Lord. He started his car and drove home.

Larry was a different story. As he entered his apartment, Larry was whistling....and shaving! "I have a date!

"With whom?"

"Sally from church."

His heart dropped into his stomach. "Jones?"

"Yes. We started talking to each other. She's divorced. Has one kid."

"And you like her? Why?"

"I'm exploring, Stanley."

"And I thought you were a confirmed bachelor."

"I was until your woman started talking to me."

"I believe she was asking you to give Holly another chance, unless I'm mistaken."

"She wants to live in the country. I'm not ready to for the country life."

Stan shook his head. Wasn't there a saying that said once a country boy always a country boy? Yes, of course! He's fighting what he truly was. "Whatever, my friend. Whatever. I'll be in my room praying."

Twenty-two

Beth wanted to do something special for Stan's birthday. Since the news about Greece, he had been a little depressed. She tried to encourage him. Waiting for change wasn't easy. He felt in his heart God called him to Greece. His birthday fell on a Friday; she would have to treat him after work.

"Lord, please keep his co-workers from razzing him or giving him a hard time." She prayed as she brushed her hair. She admired her new figure. Now at 160. She had to smile. "I look so good for Stan, Mom!"

"You always look good for him." She stood by her doorway.

"When I get to my desired weight, I'm getting a haircut." She opened her mouth at her mother's new figure. "You lost quite a bit too."

Her mother smiled as she moved her body side to side. "You like it? Are you going to the gym with me today?"

"Yes, of course. I have my gym bag ready." Her attitude had changed since she lost thirty pounds. With Stan working out too, it made a difference. When he looked at her, his eyes sparkled.

"You have plans for his birthday?"

Beth picked up her purse and followed her mom out to their cars. "I don't have any solid ideas yet. He has said my presence makes it special. Maybe I can let him take me out of town."

"I will be gone most of the day. My new love and I are going to the beach."

"How romantic!"

*****

"Wake up, birthday boy!" Larry blew out a party favor, which gave Stan a headache.

"Not now, Larry." He rolled over and pulled a pillow over his head.

"You're still upset about Greece?"

"I don't know how Beth could have such great faith. I have been praying for a month and no news."

"I think no news is good news. Keep the faith, bro."

"Would be nice if I got some good news today." He sat up, turning his back. "Not feeling up to going to the gym."

"Not even if Beth was there?"

He grinned. "How is your love life??"

Larry sat on the bed. "You're right, Stan."

"About?"

"I wasn't interested in Holly because she wanted farm life. If things proceed with us, I would have to live in the country."

"Nothing wrong with that."

"I know my old man would approve of her."

"He would."

Larry sighed. "I can't get Holly off my mind."

"Not to mention you dated her a couple of times the past month."

"Yep. So, are we ready to work out?"

Stan sat up. "I guess."

"Lunch is on me…unless Beth has plans."

"If she does, I'm not aware."

"She's looking great too! Are you going to ask her to marry you?"

"I have the ring."

"Are you going to ask her today?"

Warmth filled Stan's heart. "Yes."

"Does she have an apartment to rent? Just wondering."

"She's looking."

At the gym, Stan's heart throbbed, and he wiped his sweaty palms on his legs. He was going to ask her at the gym, but his heart raced. He scanned the room for Beth and her mother as Larry signed them both in.

"They would be in the women's section," Larry said.

Female voices alerted Stan and he smiled. The two women were none other than her mother and Beth. "Nope. Don't think so."

Beth's eyes lit up. "Hi, Stan!"

His widened, and mouth dropped open. "Wow! Look at you!"

"Weighed myself at 158," she said, proudly. "You look good too. Any news concerning Greece?"

His smile faded. "Nope."

"It will come."

"Beth," he began, "would you have dinner with me tonight?"

"I would love to!"

"Would you mind if I stop by your house?"

"No. I would love that. Do I need to dress up?"

"We're going to Olive Garden, so nothing too fancy but nice, I guess. I'll be by at 5:45. Maybe we can see a movie afterwards."

"Sounds great!"

After Larry signed them in, Stan followed him to the locker. "You're going to ask her tonight? You're going to be a bundle of nerves." Larry joked, but he was half serious.

"I'm fine. I want the date special for her."

Beth held back a giggle when Stan stood inside, looking nervous.

"Does he have any ideas?" Her mother moved up to the desk after the two men had taken off to the locker room.

Beth's heart fluttered as she caught Stan waving to her. "Not that I know of. I asked him on our last date what he would want to do on his birthday."

Beth's mother obtained the key and led her daughter to the locker room. On both side of the lockers were the shower rooms, and Larry and Stan had walked toward the men's room.

"You're watching him."

"He makes my heart sing."

Her mother nodded, and her smile warmed her heart. "I knew he would. Mother's instinct."

Beth rolled her eyes but giggled. “I have today off as usual, and I have no plans today. I hope I can spend the day with Stan.”

“Any news from Greece?”

“No and he’s discouraged. He is dissatisfied with work.”

“He should seek another job. Does he have any special skills?”

Their trainer met and led them to the equipment room. “Have you weighed yourself?”

“Yes, and I’m at 158,” Beth announced proudly.

“That’s good! Have you stayed away from carbs and sugar?”

“Sugar, yes. I have sweets occasionally but maybe a few carbs, as I still have a sandwich now and then.”

“Stay away from bleached flour and you’ll do fine. Ann?”

“I’m staying the same.” Her mother had reached her goal. She had a lot less to lose and only needed to lose fifteen pounds. She was at 125 now. Beth had such great admiration for her mother.

At the end of the workout, Beth and Stan met each other at the same time. His eyes sparkled as he lifted and kissed her hand. “Happy Birthday,” she said to him.

“Did you have a good workout?” “Exhilarating but I am beat. I’m going to take a shower and go home…. unless you have something in mind?”

“See ya later, Stan,” Larry said, waving.

“He is going to give Holly another chance.”

Beth's hand flew to her mouth and she squealed. "He is?"

"He's praying about it, but I believe he will." His eyes sparkled again.

"Believe for yourself too. God may have His reason for the delay."

He shook his head, moving in closer to her. He touched her face. "I love you, you know that?"

Her heart fluttered as he breathed his words to her. "You tell me that." Her arms found their way around Stan's lean body.

"I would like to spend the rest of the day with you, but if you have plans with your mom–"

"My mom would understand. I have your birthday gift in my car."

"You didn't have to get me anything."

"I know. I wanted to." She smiled, glancing at her mother.

"You two go ahead."

"Have fun." She headed for the exit. "See you when you get home," Ann said.

"Let me shower first."

He kissed her gently, then released her. "I need to shower too."

Fifteen minutes later, Stan exited the shower room and waited for Beth. Women tend to take a little longer, he thought. He sat in a chair and glanced around.

He hadn't thought what he would do. He bowed his head in prayer. "Lord, what would you want us to do today?" As he prayed, he remembered he hadn't invited her to his apartment. His heart raced. "Yes! I'll take her apartment hunting."

As he rose, Beth exited the shower room, wearing a white long-sleeve dress. She took his breath away. She was stunning in the dress.

"Where do we go?"

"Apartment hunting." He kissed her hand.

"I told my mom I was looking for an apartment and she looked shocked or maybe lost."

"Did she say anything?"

"No. May have been a surprise to her, but I think she understood why."

"So, are you game?"

"Yes. Why not follow me home, then we can hunt for an apartment, in your car?"

"Okay."

She gave him a huge smile. "Meet you at my house." She headed out the door.

They spent the morning driving around their town of 5,000. Beth had the newspaper in her hand while Stan kept his eyes open for any vacant signs on the windows. Hillsong came on the radio. At least he liked them. She hadn't had a chance to immerse herself in relaxing Christian music that morning, so getting her Hillsong was her fix.

"There is a house for rent five blocks from here."

He raised his eyebrows. "You want to rent a house?"

"$900 a month."

"Okay. What about bills and food. Maybe you can share a house with someone."

"Did you know Larry before you were roommates?"

"I had met him, yes."

Beth had friends, but Holly lived three miles outside of town and Julie in Montana. Holly's father was sick with cancer. Julie has Eric. She sighed. Were they her only friends? She stared out the window. "I don't know if I want to share a place with a stranger."

"I understand your thought. An apartment would be better than a house that way, but I will let you decide for yourself. Okay? Just trying to help."

"I have two friends."

"Insecurities make it hard."

"Yes."

Stan wanted to help her. Her situation weighed heavily on his heart. Over the past few months, he had seen a change on her, but not a significant one. Would moving to Greece help? God may have closed the door for Greece because she needed him. *What can I do to help her, Lord?*

The white one-story house had a For Rent sign in the front yard. It surprised him, but it shouldn't have. Beth had closed her eyes and moved her lips, and her lips were moving. Praying? Did he pressure her to move out? *Oh, Lord, I am sorry.*

She's not praying about you. I want her to pray for this house.

His skin tingled. "You do?"

"What?" Beth glanced at him.

"You're praying for the house?"

She smiled. "Yes."

He brushed her hair back. "I love a woman who prays."

Her eyes sparkled. "I love you." She reached to kiss him. "Ready?"

"Should we let them know we're coming?"

"No need to." She opened the car door.

Stan followed her to the house and waited with her as she knocked on the door. His heart froze, then pounded for this brave woman.

Another woman answered the door. "Are you here about the house?"

"Yes," Beth answered.

"Come in. Are you two married?"

His heart fluttered. Hopefully soon, he thought, but he wore a smile. "Someday. Right now, I'm her boyfriend, helping her go house shopping." He noticed the concerned look on her face.

She smiled. "Okay. Well, someone else wants to rent this house too."

Beth's heart shrunk. She had prayed that no one else would want the house. Why would the Lord not give her peace?

"Thanks for your time," Stan said.

"Not yet." Beth was waiting on the Lord. If He gave her peace, then he had an answer.

"You heard what she said."

"Maybe you two can strike a bargain," the lady suggested.

Ask for the phone number.

"Can you give me the person's phone number?

Stan's mouth dropped open.

"Sure." She went to a table and wrote down the information Beth needed.

"What's going on, Beth?"

"The Lord gave me peace. At first, I didn't understand why He would if this house was not available—" She paused. The phone rang, and the owner answered.

"Hello? Oh, yes! Hi! You changed your mind?" She glanced at Beth, who was smiling ear to ear. "No problem. Okay, bye." She hung up. The lady giggled. "I guess the house is yours. Would you like a tour?"

While Beth was beaming, Stan looked on in bewilderment. Did the Lord work a miracle? This woman completely amazed him. He shook his head in disbelief. "Yes, we would love to too."

"Yes, please."

The house had two bedrooms, two bathrooms (one in the bedroom), a small kitchen with a bar, linen closet, everything a woman could dream of, but could Beth afford the price? Stan studied her, tried to assess her mindset, and yet there seemed to be peace in her soul.

"Nine hundred a month?" Stan asked doubtfully. .

The landlady sighed. "It was fifteen hundred, but the Lord told me to lower the price. Shortly after that, people started calling, of course. And of course I had to start weeding some of them out. A few of them, like the last one, wanted it, but changed their minds."

Again, Beth was beaming. Obviously, the Lord had reserved the house for her and Stan offered his thanks to the Lord. "I guess God wants you to have this house."

"Of course, you're responsible for the electric bill."

"That's fine."

If Beth gets the house, what about Greece? He had forgotten she could go to Greece with him. Would she have to pay rent if she is not using the house? "Beth?"

She was miles ahead of him. "Where do I sign?" She wrote out a check.

Twenty-three

After an exciting morning, Stan drove Beth back to her mother's house. He didn't expect to spend his birthday this way, but he loved it. If she had any birthday gifts for him, she wouldn't have to give him anything. Seeing God work on her behalf sufficed

All that was left was for God to open the door for Greece. And his surprise later in that day.

Stan prayed as he drove them around them around town. He held her and delighted in her giggles. He loved hearing her sing worship songs by Hillsong. Why worry about Greece? If God intervened in her life as He did, He most certainly would in his life. *Forgive my unbelief, Lord.*

Stan didn't want to wait any longer. He parked his car in the Denny's parking lot. "Lunch?"

"I haven't eaten here in a while."

He smiled. "Me either."

His palm became sweaty as he fingered the ring box in his pocket. He opened the door for both him and Beth. His heart fluttered, and his stomach felt empty, yet a wave of nausea came over him.

Stan held her hand and she stared at him. "Are you nervous?"

Doubt plagued him. What if she said no? She rented a house. What if she is not ready? Relax, Stan. He took a deep breath. "You might say that." He grinned.

"What's going on with Stan?" Beth thought to herself. His palms were sweaty. In the car, he kept quiet, but smiled.

Was he planning a marriage proposal? Could she say yes? An experience Julie shared with her came to her mind. *I know he won't ask me to move in with him.* So, what else can it be? She studied him.

Stan wiped his hands on his pants as he led her into the restaurant. At the same time, he was smiling, and his eyes danced.

"How many in your party?" a hostess asked.

"Two!" Stan said.

She grabbed a couple of menus. "Smoking or nonsmoking?"

"Non," they both replied, then laughed.

The hostess smiled at their response. "Table or booth?"

"Booth," Stan said.

The hostess led them to booth close to the kitchen and gave them each a menu as they sat. "Would you like to order anything to drink?"

Beth opened the menu. "Water is fine with a slice of lemon."

Stan smiled. "The same for me." He rapped his fingers on the table. "What's next is Greece."

"If I can get a house for $900 a month, then you can be a missionary in Greece."

He stopped in mid stride, his mouth agape. "You're not coming?"

"Of course, I am—that is, if they let me. I am a new member. They may not."

He pressed his lips, but he had a twinkle in his eyes. "Well, that could change. How do you feel if you serve with me?"

Greece? At one time, she was all for going with him, until she rented a house. It couldn't be soon. She caught her breath. How could he ask her after she rented a house? It was unfair. God wouldn't send them too soon. Wait! Didn't she say they wouldn't let her? She put her fingers to her mouth.

Beads of sweat poured down his face. "I understand if you don't want to go… as my wife."

Her stomach fluttered. His wife? If yes, would he want to marry soon? She couldn't. "Stan, I–"

He pressed his lips. She had disappointed him, and he stared at the placemat. "I understand."

"I just rented a house."

"The house would still be here."

"When would we get married? No quick weddings, please."

"You have my word. Maybe six months from now."

She hated indecision, but she couldn't decide. She wanted to marry him. Six months from now? "What if you get called to Greece before then?"

"I will return, and we will marry. We'll have a honeymoon, then we will fly back to Greece."

Her lack of response gave him a headache. He prayed she would say yes, but instead she hesitated to answer. *Am I rushing her? Was I asking too soon?* As he was about to change his mind, she surprised him.

"The house was until we get married. God may have me want me to rent it for a short time. So please ask me."

He perked up and a smile built up on his face. He took the small red box out of his pocket and opened it. "Will you be my wife?"

"I would be honored to be your wife. Yes."

Warmth radiated through his body. She said yes! He immediately took the ring out and slid it over her ring finger.

Beth giggled and gave Stan a hug.

Everyone applauded as they heard her answer and Beth was flabbergasted. She never had so much attention in her life.

Stan lifted her from her seat and, as heavy as she was, swung her around.

Her head spun, and the spinning exhausted her. "You can let me down now." She giggled. "I'm impressed you did that with a 158-pound woman."

He chuckled. "I'm worm out myself." He set her down. "I got excited. I thought for a minute, more like a millisecond, that you were going to say no."

"I almost did, but God said go ahead."

He smiled wide.

Beth tried to catch her breath and she slowed down her heart. She let the proposal sink in as she stared at her ring in disbelief. *Never in my life did I attract a man who would love me for me.* Tears fell down her face. Stan was 100 times better than the last two men she dated. *Julie, you were right.* Tears wouldn't stop coming.

"Well, this definitely is the best birthday ever!"

"Congratulations." A man who was Stanley's age walked by his table.

Stanley flashed a smile. He had a woman with him who was in her twenties. "Thank you. Is she your wife?"

"Yes"

More people congratulated them and left Beth in wonderment. A photographer was there taking their picture.

Both laughed. "Now we'll be in the paper."

"Except they don't know our names." Stan fiddled with the display stand on the table.

"Yes, I will need your names," the photographer responded. "If that is okay with you."

"Stanley Powers."

Beth beamed. *Beth Powers. I love the sound of that!* She giggled. "Beth Miller."

The photographer wrote their names on a notepad. "Thanks." He left their table.

"We can discuss wedding plans tonight," Stan suggested.

"That would be best."

After lunch, they went for a drive. Beth took out her phone to call Julie. The time would be 3 p.m. in Montana. She hoped Julie would answer. If not, she would leave a message.

On the third ring, someone picked up the phone. "Hello?" Julie answered.

"Julie, it's Beth! You remember when I told you about Stan?" She smiled to Stan.

"Yes."

"We're getting married!" She squealed in abject delight.

Julie shrieked. "Eric, Beth is getting married!"

Beth giggled. Wouldn't Eric be happy for her? She could think of the witty remarks he would say. "What did she do? Wrangle him?" That remark made her laugh.

"He said congratulations. Have you set a date yet?"

"Not yet. People were congratulating us, and we decided to discuss it later today."

"Let me know when."

"Would you be my matron of honor? Oh, this means I might be leaving the states someday. I want to visit you before we do." She glanced at Stan, who was whistling and smiling.

"I would be honored, Beth! You said something about him going to Greece. Is this something you want to do?"

"Yes. I have been praying about it. I believe God was preparing me for this."

"I am happy for you."

"Thanks. So, what's new with you?"

"I'm expecting."

"What? So soon after the first baby was born?"

"Six months after baby Branson was born."

"I'm so glad you're recovering well after your rape."

"God is good. I need to get back to ranching with Eric."

"Okay. I'll let you go. Bye."

"Bye, my friend."

Beth hit end call. "One more person to tell, but I think I will take a trip to the farm."

"Don't you want to tell your mother too?"

"Of course. I'll tell her in person when I get home."

"I thought we would spend the day together…unless you want some time with your mom."

"Okay. Let me call her. Normally mom and I shop on Saturdays." She dialed her mother's number.

"Hello?"

"Mom, do you want to go shopping today?"

"Yes. Why?"

"Stan wants to spend the day together. He proposed to me!" She stared at her ring. Her heartbeat quickened and she was slowly realizing her dream. If he wanted to spend the day with her on his birthday, then why not?

"You what? Oh, Beth! That's great news! When's the big day?"

"We're going to discuss it later." She felt his arm around her.

"Right on his birthday. Okay, dear. We can shop next week. I'll help you choose a wedding dress if you like."

Beth froze. The mention of a wedding dress reminded her of her weight. She glanced at Stanley. *Oh, Lord, help me lose more weight.* "Maybe we should shop for a dress another time. We haven't discussed a date yet."

"Sure. I'll see you when you get home."

"Okay. Love you, mom." She hit end call. Beth let out an appreciative sigh. "And I love you, Stanley Powers." She gazed at him. "I can hear my mom giving her thanks to Jesus."

Stan's smile warmed her heart.

"You told me your parents are alive but divorced. Are you going to tell your mother though?"

"I will. Larry will know too. We need to pray Holly will catch your flowers." He winked.

"I agree," She chuckled.

"Have you met Holly's boyfriend?" He regarded her, yet he kept his eyes on the road.

"Clint. A couple of times. He seemed real sweet."

"It's too bad he left, but hopefully Larry will give her another chance."

"Anything can happen."

Twenty-four

Six months later.

At a svelte 135 pounds, Beth admired herself as her gown flowed elegantly down to the ground. Happy tears escaped her eyes.

"Oh, Beth! You look so radiant!" Julie's eyes glistened as she put a wrist corsage on her friend.

Beth giggled. "It's happening, isn't it?" Beth couldn't believe she was getting married. She was beyond belief.

"You better believe it," Julie responded.

More tears fell, and Beth covered her mouth with her hands.

"Someday I will marry," Holly pined.

"You will. Give Larry time."

"I want Clint back."

"You're wasting your time with him. Larry is the real deal."

"Is Larry Stan's roommate?" Julie asked.

"Was. Now Stan and I will live in my house until we are called to Greece."

"I can't believe it!" Holly said, wiping her eyes.

"How is your father?"

Holly smiled. "He's doing better."

A knock on the door. "Me."

"Come in, Eric!" Beth had asked Eric to give her away. She didn't have a father and no brothers. She didn't know who else to ask to give her away.

He opened the door and ambled in. His mouth dropped open. "Wow! Look at you!"

She giggled. "Thanks. I worked hard to get this figure, but God helped me."

"Sweetheart," said her mother, who hadn't said anything until now. "I have something for you to borrow." She gave Beth a pair of pearl drop earrings.

"Oh, Mom! Thank you!" She took out the ones she had on and replaced them with her mom's favorite earrings.

"Here is something old." Her cousin Laura pinned an heirloom brooch. "I want you to have it."

"And something new," Julie said as she gave her a diamond necklace. Beth gasped. Julie's white teeth shined. "We can afford it."

Eric added, "You deserve it."

Beth gave Julie a hug and smiled in return.

Eric checked the time on his watch. "I hear music playing. You ladies should get ready to walk down the aisle."

As the music played, Julie, Holly, and Beth's two cousins, Laura and Sarah, along with Sarah's daughter Josie, exited the dressing room.

Eric stared at Beth, and said, "I'm proud of you. You'll make an excellent wife to Stan."

"Thank you, Eric. That means a lot. I appreciate you walking me down the aisle."

"You're welcome."

Stan's heartbeat increased as he waited at the altar for his bride. Not too long ago, he didn't think he would marry anyone.

A man in his late fifties slumped in the front row pew. He scowled, but Stan tried not to let the scowl bother him. He wanted his father to see him marry. Stan offered a smile, but the older man grunted.

His mother, looking beautiful in her silver blue dress, wore her hair in a bun and a matching hat on top of her head. His mother was a queen of fashion. His father may have married her because of her fashion sense. But, unlike his father, she always wore a smile. Heat radiated in his cheeks, thinking of his mother.

Stan's two brothers, Max and Robert, waited beside him as his groomsmen. Next to them were Larry and Stan's cousin Jordan.

Stan couldn't be happier having his entire family there, but his heart saddened, knowing Beth's father could not witness the wedding.

The wedding song played. Everyone watched as the bridal party marched down the aisle elegantly. There were oohs and ahhs as the acting father escorted Beth down the aisle.

Stan's heart raced. He banished all thoughts to ditch the bride at the altar and he was having no second thoughts. He loved her as Christ loved her. He smiled wide as the bride reached the altar and gazed at him under her veil.

Epilogue

One Sunday morning, the Mr. and Mrs. Powers prepared for church. Stan zipped up Beth's dress before he finished his tie.

"Good morning, my dear." He kissed her face.

"Sleep well?" She asked.

"Not really. I had visions last night. I have peace and confidence that we'll leave for Greece soon."

She parted her mouth. "You do?"

He smiled. "Yes. I feel it in the air."

"After six months of marriage, we finally leave for Greece?"

"Are you excited?" He asked.

"Nervous."

"Don't be."

They finished dressing and Stan took his Bible, his keys, and he turned off lights as he led his beautiful bride to his white car.

"I love being married to you! Life is an adventure with you." She gazed into his blue eyes.

"Same here." He kissed her lips, then opened the door for her.

Nothing unusual happened as they entered the sanctuary. The greeters welcomed them and said hello as they handed them a bulletin.

Stan led Beth to their favorite pew. The same pew she chose when she became a member of the church. This time Larry was not there because he was attending service with Holly. Stan felt warm inside. The Powers had prayed Holly would choose Larry and that he would accept her rural way of life. Once a country girl always a country girl.

The Pastor headed their way and bent down to Stan's level. "Good news. You not giving up on Greece has paid off. Meet me in my office after service."

Beth gasped. "Oh, Stanley!"

All his limbs relaxed. His chest expanded and his face warmed. It overwhelmed him in a good way. How could he repay God? He beamed. "If it wasn't for your great faith." He planted a kiss on her lips.

"You had to believe too." "I know. Thanks for supporting me." As he held her hand, his heart fluttered.

"You're welcome."

The End

A Note of Thanks

Dear Reader, I hoped you enjoyed A Man for Beth. If you have, please do me a favor. Go to where you downloaded this book and write a good and honest review for me. **It is very much appreciated!** If you haven't already, you can download my first book in the series which is free. Also feel free to email me at rmadison_1@hotmail.com (r before m) or use the contact form at my website. I would love to hear from you!

If you are struggling with your weight and your identity, know that Jesus loves you. If you are born again, then your identity is in Jesus Christ. If you don't have a relationship with him, and you would like one, click on this link

https://www.intouch.org/read/how-do-i-accept-jesus-as-my-savior

Acknowledgements

I would not have written this book if God had not given me the ability to write. To him, I give the praise and glory for the inspiration of this story. I also want to acknowledge my lovely sister who has been my biggest supporter and my sounding board.

Even when I felt alone, I knew I wasn't alone. My sister Elizabeth Derby is not only my sister and support system, but she is my best friend next to Jesus. I also like to thank you readers for taking the time to read my stories and leaving reviews for me. And lastly, but not least Carmen DeSousa for telling me about her awesome editor Robert Helle. I could not have gotten this book published and for you to read without his help.

About the Author

Ruthie Madison doesn't just write romance. She writes whatever God inspires to write. Her first book was born out of her trials in Hanford, Ca. Its storyline was not liked by many so she took it down and is in middle of major revising. The book is entitled, **A Second Chance at Love.** Following that she has a written a series (This is the third in the series): See below for other books by Ruthie Madison. Other than writing, she also design book covers. You may have seen some of them on your favorite author books. Check out her website which is in the front of the book. Ruthie Madison enjoys crocheting, worshipping Jesus and early morning time with her sister. She is survived by her mother who recently passed away in December of 2017

Also in the Second Chance Series

The Past Hunter: When the Past Comes Calling

Baby Blues

Also by Ruthie Madison

Purify My Heart

A Christian Horror

Made in the USA
Monee, IL
18 October 2026

66035040R00104